"Savy asked me to play lead in the pit band. I told her no way."

"I think you should do it," I said casually, leaning against a locker.

"Oh, yeah?" Wyatt asked. Slowly he put his hand on the wall over my head and leaned in toward me. "How come?"

I could smell his toothpaste, and something deliciously musky, like patchouli oil. The little hairs on the back of my neck tingled. *You are in love with Chad,* I reminded myself. "Because you're a good player, and if you play lead we'll have a good pit band," I said simply.

"You want me to do it?" he asked me in a low voice, leaning in even closer to me.

"Yeah," I squeaked, then cleared my throat. "I mean, sure, if you want to," I added as casually as I could.

"So what will you do for me in return?" he asked me, a lazy, insinuating smile playing at the corners of his mouth.

"Drum so good that you'll sound decent for a change," I replied, giving him a bored look. I couldn't let him see me sweat. . . .

WILD HEARTS

CHERIE BENNETT

AN ARCHWAY PAPERBACK
Published by POCKET BOOKS
New York   London   Toronto   Sydney   Tokyo   Singapore

AN ARCHWAY PAPERBACK *ORIGINAL*

An Archway Paperback published by
POCKET BOOKS, a division of Simon & Schuster Inc.
1230 Avenue of the Americas, New York, NY 10020

Copyright © 1994 by Cherie Bennett

ISBN: 0-671-86513-7

First Archway Paperback printing February 1994

10 9 8 7 6 5 4 3 2 1

AN ARCHWAY PAPERBACK and colophon are
registered trademarks of Simon & Schuster Inc.

Cover photos by Michel LeGrou/Media Photo Group

Printed in the U.S.A.

IL: 7+

For Jeff

CHAPTER 1

It is a simple fact of life: most parents are excruciating.

My father, for example, a man with a reasonable three-digit IQ, wears black nylon socks with sandals. In public. My mother, a woman who can speak four languages fluently, talks baby talk to my father when she wants something from him. He finds this charming.

I think I've made my point.

And yet, compared to my friends' parents, mine are better than most. That's what I *thought*, anyway, until they made the Big Announcement that clearly was going to ruin my life.

Maybe things were just going too well. We lived in a very cool apartment on the Upper West Side of Manhattan. I was about to begin my junior year at the High School of Performing Arts, where I had a reputation as the best drummer in the school. Guys think a girl drummer is a very hip thing, which might be how I had attracted the coolest guy in the school, Chad Berman, as my boyfriend.

Now, I am reasonably cute, but I am not mega-cute, if you know what I mean. I have brown hair and brown eyes, and I'm about average height and weight, which would make me hideously normal if it weren't for my talent on the drums. That made me special, set me apart, and I dreamed dreams of musical greatness that could actually come true.

In short, I had a perfect life. Chad—he plays lead guitar and sings—and I had a band, The Chill, and we were already playing around at places like CBGB's. I had great friends, great style—I create my own fashions, usually from thrift shops—great talent, a great boyfriend, and I lived in New York City. I ask you, what more could a sixteen-year-old girl want?

And then came that fateful day when my parents sat me and my fourteen-year-old sister, Jill, down at our kitchen table for the Big Announcement.

"Well, kids, we have a family decision to make," my father said cheerfully, swiping absent-mindedly at his bald spot.

"A really exciting one," my mother added.

Sha, right. Whenever my parents call a family meeting and say we have a family decision to make, it invariably means they are about to tell me I have to do something I'm not going to want to do and we're all going to pretend to vote on it.

"Great!" my little sister said eagerly. I shot her a look of pure loathing. Jill has blond hair and blue eyes and is a cheerleader. She likes to pretend she is an airhead even though she isn't. She is also the biggest suck-up in the world.

"Well, there are some really interesting changes going on at work," my father began. "A lot of expansion, a lot of opportunities."

I nodded guardedly. My father is an executive at Nissan Motors. He actually likes his job. If I had to go to some office every day and make such monumental decisions as what color the new car line should be, I would slit my wrists. Dad, however, lives for this sort of thing.

"Anyway," he continued, "I've been offered a major promotion."

"Major," Mom echoed significantly.

"My new title will be senior vice president of marketing," he continued, "and it means a really substantial raise."

"Can I get a car?" Jill asked hopefully.

3

"You're fourteen," I reminded her. "You can't drive yet."

"Okay, how about my own phone?" she wheedled.

"We'll see," Mom said.

This is, of course, parent-speak for no.

"Well, I'm really happy for you, Daddy," Jill said, throwing her arms around my father's neck and kissing his cheek.

"Why do I feel like I'm waiting for the other shoe to fall here?" I asked, fiddling with one of the six earrings in my right ear.

"There is one more thing," my father admitted anxiously. "This new position would force us to move."

"To . . . ?" Jill asked expectantly.

Dad looked at Mom.

"Nashville, Tennessee!" Mom announced, as if we had just won the lottery.

I stared at my parents. "Run that by me again," I suggested.

"Dad's new job involves our moving to Nashville, Tennessee," my mom explained.

"Is that, like, actually in the United States?" I asked dryly.

"Wow," Jill breathed. "Isn't that where Scarlett O'Hara grew up?"

"I think that's Atlanta, dear," my mother said absentmindedly.

"So, we're supposed to be voting on moving to Nashville, Tennessee?" I asked.

Dad nodded. "I know this would be a really big change for this family," he said. "That's why we've got to decide together."

"Well, I vote no. Case closed," I said.

Dad reached over and touched my hand. "I need your support here, babe," he said quietly.

"No coercing the voters," I snapped, pulling my hand away. He had a hangdog look on his face. "Dad! You can't expect me to give up my entire life because you got a promotion!"

"I don't think you'd be giving up your life," my mother said. "Maybe Tennessee would be great fun."

"Well, I'm not going," I said flatly, folding my arms.

"Jill?" my father asked.

"I'm happy for you, Daddy," Jill said. "It sounds like an adventure!"

Mom looked at me. "I vote yes, too," she told me.

I looked at all three of them, staring at me. "See, this is what always happens! No one ever votes with me!" I cried. "You are making a mockery out of the democratic process!"

"It's a perfectly fair system," my mother pointed out.

"No, it isn't," I insisted. "You two always vote

together, and Jill hasn't had an original thought in her life!"

"I have, too!" Jill insisted.

"Well, I'm not going," I repeated.

"Honey, we're a family—" my father began.

"And one member of this family isn't going to Nashville!" I stood up angrily. "I'll stay with Chad."

"No, you will not stay with Chad," my father said in a steely voice.

"Okay, with one of my girlfriends, then," I amended, realizing the stay-with-Chad idea had not exactly gone over well. "Anita. Or Debbie."

"I don't think Anita's parents or Debbie's want another kid moving in with them," Jill pointed out.

This was undoubtedly true. "Well, I'll get my own apartment, then," I insisted. "You can make me an emancipated minor." This was a shot in the dark—I was pretty sure that meant you could live on your own and be under eighteen.

"You're too young to have your own apartment," Jill said righteously.

"I am not!" I screamed. I knew I sounded childish, but I just couldn't help myself.

"Sweetie, I know you don't want to move," my mom said gently. "I understand it's a sacrifice for you. But we're a family. And families stick together."

No way out. No way out.

"I bet there are fabulous musicians in Nashville," my mother added. "You'll like that."

"*Country* music?" I asked in a withering voice. "You think I'm going to hang out with *country* musicians?"

"Well, isn't a good musician a good musician?" Dad asked reasonably.

I wanted to scream or cry or just kill someone. "God, you don't understand anything!" I ranted. I ran to my room and slammed my door shut and threw myself on my bed. Then I reached over and turned my stereo up as loud as it would go.

But no matter how much I tried to drown everything out, the awful, hideous truth was still there: there was no way out.

I was moving to Nashville, Tennessee.

My life was over.

"Don't you just love the way they talk here?" Jill asked me in the dark.

"Oh, yeah, it's ducky," I said sarcastically, staring up at what would be the ceiling if I could see.

A mere three weeks after that family meeting, we had indeed moved to Nashville, Tennessee. My parents had decided to build a house in a subdivision called Greenhills Estates, and so we had moved into a hideous two-bedroom apartment in a complex called Sunny Acres. Tell me that doesn't sound like a home for old people who can't remember their names. Sunny Acres has a swimming pool and a hot tub where teens hang out drinking beer from the can in a futile attempt to look cool. I always picked a lounge chair as far away from them as was humanly possible and spent my days with my head buried in some novel by Ayn Rand, the longer and more depressing the better.

Jill, in her new yellow bikini, made friends with them all right away. It was as if she had been holding her breath for fourteen years, just waiting to become an instant southern belle. By our second week there she was throwing the occasional "y'all" into her conversation and wearing dresses with flowers and little lace collars. It was like watching *Invasion of the Body Snatchers*. New York Jill, whom I knew and even occasionally loved, had been replaced by Southern Belle Jill, who was indescribably icky. Not only was she still a suck-up, she was now a southern suck-up.

As for me, I was, as predicted, completely miserable. I wrote to Chad daily, ran up long-distance phone bills to my friends, and generally cried myself to sleep.

Finally the night before the first day of school was upon us. Jill already had an outfit picked out, which lay across the chair by the dresser: a pink T-shirt and a little pink flowered skirt with a matching hair ribbon. I was planning to swathe myself in black, befitting my mood.

"Don't you think that Jimmy Lee guy who hangs out at the pool is cute?" Jill asked me from across our darkened bedroom.

"Is he the one who rhymes 'tinsel' and 'pencil'?" I asked sarcastically.

Jill giggled. "Isn't it cute? He calls me Jilly. And he calls Mom 'ma'am'! He grew up on a farm. Did you know that?"

"And had a close personal relationship with various attractive sheep, no doubt," I murmured.

"Ha! It was a tobacco farm. There weren't any sheep," Jill said triumphantly.

"Oh, good, his family is personally responsible for giving cancer to thousands of people," I replied.

"No one forces anyone else to smoke," Jill said righteously. "That's what Jimmy Lee says."

"Hey, it's the American way," I mumbled, beating my pillow into a better position.

"You know, you might have fun here if you would give it half a chance," my sister whispered.

"Jill, trust me: I will never have fun here," I replied. "I hate it here. And the very instant I graduate from Hocum High—"

"Green Hills High," Jill corrected me.

"Yeah, whatever," I said. "The instant I'm out of there I will go back to New York. Then I will hire a hypnotist to erase these two years from my memory, and I will resume my real life. And I will pretend that Nashville, Tennessee, never, ever happened to me."

CHAPTER
2

💮

I was stuck in a nightmare.

That first day of school my mother dropped Jill off in front of Green Hills Middle School and then dropped me off in front of Green Hills High. As I walked toward the front door of the building my ears were assaulted by overheard snatches of inane conversation.

"Did y'all see how *cute* Bubba Thatcher got over the summer? I swear he's to *die* for now!"

"Well, I don't *care* if Sue Ellen Whitley got religion. She's still trash and she'll *never* get homecoming queen!"

"Y'all, I am going to *perish* if I don't make cheerleader this year. I mean it, I will *perish!*"

I am not exaggerating. This is really the way they talked.

I looked straight ahead, desperately wishing I was some place—any place—else. All around me gaggles of blond-haired girls were shrieking together, hugging, laughing. They were dressed like variations on a theme—pastel skirt and flowered top or flowered skirt and pastel top with matching hair ribbons. I myself did not own a garmento in a pastel shade, nor would I have been caught dead in one. For the first day of school I had chosen a black leather miniskirt over black leggings and ancient black motorcycle boots with silver studs. On top I wore my favorite Boy Scout shirt, acquired at the Salvation Army for $2.00; it had a merit badge in wildlife skills sewn on the shoulder—that appealed to me. Over that I wore a sleeveless jean jacket upon which my former best friend from when I still had a life, Anita Lebowitz, had hand-painted a portrait of Jim Morrison on fire. To top things off, I wore a backward baseball cap with the legend "Born to Die Young" on the brim. I considered adding a veil, since I was in heavy mourning for my former life, but I figured some teacher would just make me take it off. Why give them that kind of leverage?

As I walked down the hall toward the room number I'd been given as my homeroom on a computer printout, I noticed kids stopping in mid-conversation to stare at me. Then they'd whisper to each other. And then they'd stare at me some more.

"Who *is* that?" I heard one girl hiss to another.

"Can you *believe* that outfit?" another girl said, shuddering.

I stared straight ahead, pretending not to notice, not to care. I thought about all of my friends back in New York. I thought about Chad and our band. I thought about how everyone considered my outfits hip and incredibly cool. A huge lump came to my throat. I, Jane McVay, the best drummer at the High School of Performing Arts in New York City, had been sentenced to purgatory.

"Welcome to homeroom!" the teacher, a Ms. Langley, chirped at us after the bell rang. I knew her name was Ms. Langley because she'd written it on the blackboard in big block letters. She had a fresh-scrubbed face and wore an outfit much like every girl in the class, right down to the matching mint-green hair ribbon. "I'm new here at Green Hills High this year, and I am just thrilled to death that school is actually starting! I've been marking the days on my calendar, because . . . well, this is my first teaching job!"

Gee, who would have guessed?

"I'll be teaching phys. ed. and Family Living, and I hope to see some of y'all as my students!" Ms. Langley exclaimed.

I looked down at my printout of classes. There it was—third period, Family Living with Ms. Langley. I had no idea what Family Living was, but all juniors were required to take it. Ms. Langley took attendance, went over more business in a perky fashion, and then we left for our first class.

I will save you the agony of hearing about my first three classes of the day—World Lit, chemistry, and the infamous Family Living—which were basically boring. I was surprised to find that the homework got piled on right away. The kids really paid attention in class, too. My parents had told me that Green Hills High was supposed to be so academically excellent that even the richest families sent their kids there instead of to private school.

Frankly, I had never been particularly interested in academics, so I wasn't really psyched to see the heavy workload we were expected to carry. I listened in class, wrote stuff down, walked from classroom to classroom. A lot of people stared at me, but no one spoke to me. I felt as if I had just arrived from another planet, and I fervently wished to be beamed back home.

I did notice a really pretty black girl in my history class who clearly was very smart. She'd done advanced reading in the summer and asked questions about the American Revolution that were really astute. She even wore a reasonably normal-looking outfit of jeans and a pressed denim shirt. Her name was Sandra. I overheard someone say she was president of the junior class. She was the first person who smiled at me in a genuinely friendly way instead of smiling like she was just being polite while actually thinking I was the weirdest thing of all time.

After lunch—a sordid little experience in a cafeteria where I sat by myself and spooned yogurt into my mouth for a half hour—I knew I would be facing the most depressing of all my classes. It was called Advanced Jazz Band, and was my elective. I knew it would be depressing because I knew that the musicians would suck. I figured they would play some stupid, simple little ditties and pretend it was jazz.

My mother had talked me into taking this elective. "You can't just let your music go," she'd said to me. I had reluctantly agreed, but now that I was walking down the hall to Advanced Jazz Band, I had a terrible, sinking feeling that I'd rather never play the drums again than sit through the torture I knew I was about to face.

"Okay, people, find a seat," the teacher called as kids milled around talking with each other. I sat in the back and got my first surprise of the day: the teacher had on cool clothes. She wore black jeans, a black sleeveless mock turtleneck, and black cowboy boots. Her hair was long and dark brown with nary a hair ribbon in sight.

I looked around at the twenty or so kids in the room and got my second surprise: these kids did not all look the same. There was an Asian girl, a tall black guy, and the black girl, Sandra, from my history class. There were three guys with really long hair; two had diamond studs in their left ear. And while some of the girls in the room were dressed in those lame flowery outfits, others were dressed in jeans, minis, hippie-looking lace vests, all kinds of things.

"I'm happy to see you all again," the teacher continued, her eyes scanning the room. "We've got two new members of the band this year"— she looked down at a sheet of paper—"Mark Pepperdine and Jane McVay. Could the two of you raise your hands?"

From the other side of the room a hand shot up, attached to a boy whose abundant zits looked like a relief map. I rolled my eyes and lifted one finger laconically, then dropped my hand back into my lap.

"Welcome," the teacher said, smiling at both of us. "I'm Sharon Jacobi. The kids in this band have already played together for a year, so why don't the two of you tell us something about yourselves? Mark?"

"Yes, ma'am," Mark said, standing up next to

his desk. He cleared his throat. "My family just moved up here from Mississippi," he continued in an accent so thick I wasn't sure he was actually speaking English. His zits turned a bright red from embarrassment. "I was in jazz band at my other school," he added. "I play bass." He sat back down.

Ms. Jacobi nodded at him as if he had actually said something of interest, then she turned to me. "Jane?"

"Drums," I said tersely.

Ms. Jacobi laughed. "Could I pry a little more info out of you? I think the others would be really interested in your background."

"I just moved here from New York. I was going to the High School of Performing Arts. As soon as I graduate from here I will be going back to New York," I concluded in a bored voice.

"Did any of you ever see the movie *Fame?*" Ms. Jacobi asked the class. A few people nodded. "Well, that movie was about the school Jane went to. It's a special high school for kids who are gifted performers. Jane had to audition to get accepted. The competition is really fierce." Some kids looked over at me with interest. "We're really excited about having you in our band this year," she added.

Well, I'm certainly not really excited to be here, I thought to myself, folding my arms in front of me defensively. So what if she was nice? I knew the band was going to suck—and if there is one thing I cannot stand it is amateur musicians.

"So, how about if we jam a little to warm up?" Ms. Jacobi suggested, nodding toward the various instruments across the room. People moved quickly—a cute, small, plump redhead wearing shocking pink jean overalls went to the piano, Sandra took out a flute, one of the cute long-haired guys plugged in a Stratocaster. Okay, so he could afford a cool guitar. That didn't mean he could actually play the thing. No one went to sit behind the drums—a very nice set, I noted.

"Our drummer moved out of town," the teacher told me. "Are you ready to step in?"

I shrugged and took a seat behind the drums.

"Any suggestions?" Ms. Jacobi asked.

" 'Jelly Jam'?" the cute girl at the piano suggested.

Ms. Jacobi looked over at me. "You cool with that?" she asked me.

"Yeah," I said. "Jelly Jam" is a jazz standard in syncopated rhythm that happens to be really difficult to play. These kids were going to start with "Jelly Jam"?

"One, two, one, two, three, four," the girl at the piano counted off. Then she played the opening riff that led into the opening melody.

I came in on cue, keeping a steady beat. I

added some flourishes, a few original touches, but I held back, not showing off. After the first verse and chorus everyone dropped out but me and the keyboard player. I knew this was the point where musicians took solo turns, improvising on the melody line, accompanied by the drummer on a simple backbeat.

So this girl at the piano began her solo. And she was good. I mean she was really, *really* good. No one in the room seemed particularly impressed, though kids nodded and bopped to the rhythm and gave her a round of applause when she finished.

Next Sandra took a solo on her flute. And she was amazing. Really amazing. Her tone was clear, her style fluid, her runs super. She was as good as the best flutists at the High school of Performing Arts.

The cute guy on lead guitar was next. He was good, but not as good as Chad.

"Take it, Jane," Ms. Jacobi called to me as the guitarist finished his solo.

I did. I couldn't resist showing off a little. I did a dazzling solo line and finished with a flourish. Some kids in the room whooped and whistled when I finished.

All the musicians came back in. We went through the chorus again and finished the tune.

After that we played standard after standard. Then we switched to rock, and if anything, the musicians were even better on rock tunes. It was almost, sort of, actually . . . fun. But too soon the hour was up. I would have to leave this sanctuary and return to the land of the pastel people.

"Hey, you're really good," Sandra said to me as she cleaned off and put away her flute.

"Thanks," I said. "You too."

"I'm Sandra Farrell," she told me, gathering up her books. "Don't call me Sandy."

"Jane McVay. Don't call me Janie."

Sandra Don't-Call-Me-Sandy laughed. "Welcome," she said, nodding at me briskly. "You're a great addition to the band."

"Hi, I'm Savy Leeman," the little redhead who played keyboard said, rushing over to me. "It's short for Savannah. Listen, you are really incredible!"

I admit it, I was pleased. "Thanks," I said.

"That solo you did on 'Heat Wave' was awesome!"

"I like rock oldies," I told her.

"Oh, me too," Savy exclaimed. "But my favorite is country."

I made a face and gathered up my schoolbooks.

Savy laughed and fell in beside me as we walked out the door. "Hey, you're in Nashville now," she pointed out. "You have to like country!"

"No, I don't."

She laughed again. "A lot of the kids in the band have parents who are professional musicians around town," she explained. "Country music pays the bills."

"But country is just so . . . so lame," I protested.

"Well, maybe you just haven't really been introduced to it right," Savy said. "Hey, you'll have to come over sometime and play with my family. Everyone in my family plays country—the real thing," she added.

"Take her up on it," the girl who'd been playing the clarinet said when she overheard Savy. "Her older twin brothers are to die for."

Savy laughed. "She's right, they are, although they are also a pain in the butt. Anyway, we'll set something up, okay?"

"Whatever," I replied coolly.

"Great!" Savy said, enthusiasm spilling out of her. "I gotta run and return my friend's psych book to her. See ya!"

I watched Savy Leeman running down the hall. I couldn't decide if she was really nice or if her enthusiasm was too icky.

"Oh, hey!" she called to me, turning around and running backward. "I love your outfit!"

Okay. She was really nice.

CHAPTER
3
♡

*M*om picked Jill and me up after school, and we returned to our apartment in Sunny Acres. Somehow the local junior bubbas had beat us home and were already splashing in the pool, showing off for tittering girls in teeny bathing suits.

"I can't wait to go for a swim," Jill said, interrupting her rhapsody about how great the first day of school had been just long enough to wave to her new buddies at the pool.

Back in our tiny shared room I watched her change into a pink and white polka-dot bikini with little pink frills over each thigh. She had purchased it two days earlier at the Green Hills Mall.

"You really don't miss New York at all?" I

asked her as she brushed her blond hair and tied it back with a pink ribbon.

"Well, I miss my friends," Jill admitted. "But I think Nashville is just great!"

I took off my sleeveless denim vest and hung it over a chair. Then I stretched out on my bed. "But how can you just ... pick up your life and change everything?" I asked her. I really, truly wanted to know how she did it—how she could be so happy when I was so miserable.

"Gee, I don't know," she said with a shrug, slipping on a pink fishnet bathing suit cover-up that didn't cover anything up. "Maybe, unlike *someone* I know, I am open to new experiences."

"Or maybe you just have the sensitivity of a mothball," I suggested.

She flipped her ponytail at me. "Just keep in mind that if you are as hateful to the kids at school as you are to me, you are not going to be very popular."

"Jill, I don't want to be popular," I said in a level voice.

She stared at me coolly. "Call me Jilly. I think it's cuter." Then she picked up her aloe suntan gel and bopped out of the apartment.

I changed into cutoffs and wandered back into the kitchen, grabbing some juice from the fridge. Mom started right in grilling me about my first day, her face shiny with expectation. I still felt so angry at not being back home with my friends that I didn't tell her about the only good thing— jazz band. I told her all the awful stuff, though, ran her through every excruciating minute.

"Maybe if you *tried* to fit in," she suggested tentatively, pushing a plate of cookies at me like a peace offering.

"Jill is definitely your daughter," I muttered.

"What is that supposed to mean? Of course Jill is my daughter!"

"Mom, I don't want to fit in," I explained with exasperation. "That's the whole point!"

"They can't all be bad," my mother said. "It isn't logical."

I stood up, picked up my books, and headed for my room. My mother would never understand. She is basically a very nice person, and so is my father, but they are both people who believe in—and live by—the art of "fitting in." Like I should go through life like a chameleon, like I should achieve some kind of protective coloration so I wouldn't stand out, be different. Like being original wasn't the only way I could even begin to figure out who I was. I lay on my bed, opened my history book, and contemplated the Civil War—or the War between the States, as some Daughter of the Confederacy in bilious mint green lace had insisted it was really called.

About two hours later my mom knocked on

my door and popped her head in. I was almost through with my history homework.

She smiled and handed me a large bag that read "Castner Knott."

"What's this?" I asked.

"Just a little present," she said, sitting next to me on the bed.

I opened the bag and pulled out a yellow and white striped T-shirt with white rickrack around the sleeves. With it was a matching yellow skirt with flowers on the pockets in the same yellow and white stripes. And yes, there in the bottom of the bag was a yellow and white hair bow.

"You're not serious," I said.

She smiled tentatively. "I just thought ..."

"You didn't really think I'd wear these things—"

"I just thought ..." she said again, her hands going all fluttery.

I swallowed hard. How could my own mother not know me at all? "Listen, I know you meant well, Mom," I said, "but I would never—"

"It would look so pretty on you," Mom implored me, "and you might feel more ... more ..."

"I know you want me to fit in and be happy," I interrupted, pushing the yellow horror back into the bag. "But walking around dressed like lawn furniture isn't going to do it. Fitting in will never make me happy."

"Oh, honey," my mom said, "fitting in makes everyone happy."

"No," I told her, glancing over at my denim sleeveless jacket, at Jim Morrison on fire painted on the back. "It really doesn't."

"So this guy—his name is Brendan Mantroy, but everyone calls him Junior—he's captain of the middle school football team, and he's really, really cute, and he comes up to me and he goes, 'You look just like some movie actress, I can't think of her name.' Isn't that awesome?" My sister shoveled another spoonful of delicious, nutritious oatmeal into her mouth and took a dainty sip of orange juice.

"Gag me," I muttered under my breath. I took a sip of black coffee, and my mother shot me a look that said, "Be nice."

I didn't feel like being nice. It was seven-thirty the next morning. We were having breakfast in something the apartment brochure had referred to as a "dining nook," and I was about to have my mother drive me to my second day of school at Hocum High. If I were back in New York, I would be getting on the subway with my friends. I would be laughing and happy, I would be kissing Chad between subway stops.

"Please, at least have some fruit with that coffee, honey," my mother said.

"I'm not hungry," I replied.

Dad lowered the *Tennessean* and scowled at me. "Eat something," he commanded.

I picked up a piece of toast and ostentatiously took a bite.

"Thank you," he said, putting down the paper. He looked me over and squinted. "Do kids dress like that here?" he asked me.

I had on jeans about four sizes too big, bunched up at my waist with a pair of Mickey Mouse suspenders. On top I wore a man's T-shirt, and over that I wore a ruffled midi-vest covered with tiny pieces of plastic fruit. My shoes were cork platform sandals with little cherries that shook when I walked.

"I do," I replied.

"Well, it was fine in New York—" my father began.

"Don't start on me," I warned him. "I'm the same person. If it wasn't for you I'd still be in New York."

"That's true," he said with a sigh. He straightened his red striped tie that was too short and looked over at my mother. "Did you tell her the good news?"

"You tell," my mother said with a smile.

"I know you're not very happy here," my father said. "I know you don't want your mother driving you to school every day. So I've decided to buy the two of you girls a car."

Huh? This *was* good news. And I had actually taken a driver training course the year before, even though nobody I knew in Manhattan actually drove a car.

"Obviously Jill can't drive it yet, but you'll share the car when she gets her license," my father finished.

"Oh, Daddy!" Jill said, jumping up to throw her arms around our father's neck. "What kind?"

"A Nissan Sentra," my father said, hugging her back. "You guys can pick out the color."

"Pink!" Jill cried.

"Black," I insisted. "And I pick because you can't drive it for two years."

"It's still half mine," she reminded me.

"We'll pick it out together this weekend," my father promised. He looked over at me. "So doesn't that deserve at least a smile?"

I smiled. "Thanks, really," I said. Now I would have wheels. If only I had some place to go.

"Jane! Hey, Jane! Over here!"

I looked around the crowded cafeteria and saw Savy Leeman waving at me from a table near the back of the room. I carried my tray over.

"Hi! Have a seat!" she offered, sliding over one.

"Thanks," I said, sitting down next to her.

"This is Kimmy Carrier," Savy said, nodding at a girl across from us. The girl was very thin, very blond, and even sitting down she seemed very tall. Her eyes were pale blue, magnified behind thick glasses. I thought she was kind of great-looking, like some kind of rare, exotic pale flower. She barely glanced up at me, then lowered her eyes again.

"Hi," I said, reaching for my yogurt.

"Kimmy and I have been friends forever," Savy continued. "Right, Kim?"

Kimmy nodded and pushed some cottage cheese around on her plate.

"Honestly, Kimmy, you never eat," said Savy, chiding her friend. She looked over at me spooning out my yogurt. "Yuck," she said, making a face. "I hate that stuff." She took a big bite of a tuna fish sandwich on thick, dark rye bread. It looked delicious. "My grandmother," she explained. "She makes all of our lunches every morning. She likes to do it. She thinks we'll get poisoned otherwise!"

"She lives with you?" I asked, stirring the strawberries in the bottom of the carton.

Savy nodded. "She's a hoot. She is totally convinced that we're all going to hell because we don't keep kosher."

I looked up at Savy with surprise.

"You're Jewish?"

"Yep," she replied, licking some tuna off her finger. "Why, are you?"

"No, but a lot of my friends back home are. My boyfriend, Chad, is half Jewish, and by best friend, Anita Lebowitz, is conservative. I went to her bat mitzvah three years ago," I added.

"Don't remind me," Savy groaned. "I had to study Hebrew forever! I didn't have any time for my music!"

"It seems weird," I said contemplatively. "I mean, you have a southern accent and you're Jewish."

"It is possible to be both, you know," Savy said. "Wait until you hear Hebrew with a southern accent. It's a panic!" She gulped down the last of her sandwich. "So listen, I've got this fabulous idea." She glanced over at Kimmy, who looked skittish. "It *is* a fabulous idea, Kimmy," she insisted.

"I don't think so," Kimmy whispered.

Savy sighed. "My friend Kimmy here is a truly kick-butt lead guitar player," Savy began.

"I am not," Kimmy protested.

"You are!" Savy insisted. "Her older brother taught her, and now she's way better than he is!"

"So why aren't you in jazz band?" I asked Kimmy.

"Oh, I never could!" she whispered in horror,

as if I had just suggested that she, say, moon the principal's office just for the fun of it.

"Of course you could," Savy replied, "if you wanted to."

"Okay, then, I don't want to," Kimmy said in her tiny voice.

Savy turned to me. "She won't play in front of anybody but me," she explained.

"Ever?" I asked.

"Ever so far," Savy added. "I was just telling her about you—how great you are on the drums—and I was saying that it would be totally cool if the two of you came over on Sunday and played with my family."

"Your family all play?" I wondered.

Savy nodded. "Even my little brother, Timmy, plays the spoons; he's only six. Gramma Beth plays the fiddle. She can switch from Jewish folk songs to get-down country on a dime."

"Gee . . ." I said, at a loss for words.

"The twins play Autoharp and drums, Daddy plays bass, Mom plays flute and oboe, my little sister, Shelaylah, plays slide guitar, and she's a hellified clogger."

"Clogger?" I asked, beginning to feel overwhelmed.

"You don't know how to clog?" Savy asked. "Oh, well, Shelly loves to teach people. Anyway, we do this musical thing every Sunday, and I really want the two of you to come! Gramma Beth makes a feast—part Russian, part southern—you have to eat it to believe it."

I felt dizzy. "How many people are in your family?"

"Eight, counting Gramma Beth," Savy replied. She kicked Kimmy under the table. "So, you up for it?"

"I can't do it, Savy," Kimmy insisted.

"But, Kimmy," Savy protested. "You are good. Better than good. You're great! What good is it being a great guitar player if you never play in front of anyone?"

Kimmy nervously pushed her glasses up her nose. "I will play . . . eventually. But I'm not ready."

Savy groaned. "You are driving me bonkers, Kimmy."

Kimmy just shrugged and mushed her cottage cheese.

"Well, are you up for it?" she asked me. "I already told my family all about you!"

I was flattered as well as surprised. "I don't play country," I warned her.

Savy laughed and stood up with her tray. "Oh, you just *think* you don't play country," she corrected me. "By the time my family is through with you, you'll be a fool for that high, lonesome sound."

"Never happen," I replied with certainty, gathering up my stuff.

"Never say never!" Savy replied with a laugh. "You are about to be introduced to the Leeman household."

"It's an experience," Kimmy said in a soft voice, throwing her cottage cheese plate into the trash.

That turned out to be the understatement of a lifetime.

CHAPTER
4

♡

Shouldn't you take something?" my mother asked, hovering over me as I finished breakfast on Sunday morning. "A plant?"

"No, Mom," I said patiently, popping a section of orange into my mouth.

"But you want to make a good impression—"

"Mom, kids don't take plants to each other's houses. Savy would think it was geeky."

"Okay." She nodded, pulling a chair up next to me. She smiled and lovingly pushed some hair behind one of my ears.

I hate my hair that way, but I resisted the impulse to pull it back. I didn't want her to feel insulted. She was just so *thrilled* that someone from Hocum High had actually invited me over.

She just wanted so *badly* for me to be happy. To fit in.

"Savy is just the cutest name," my mother continued. "Short for ... ?"

"Savannah," I said.

"Savannah," my mother repeated. "Well, that is very darling. Is she a really nice girl?"

"How would I know? I barely know her," I snapped, unable to stop myself. My mother's neediness on my behalf felt like an itchy mohair sweater with too tight a neckline.

"I need a ride to the mall," Jill called out as she came into the kitchen. "I'm meeting my friends there in a half hour." She got some orange juice out of the fridge.

"Excuse me, Jill, but I'm not your personal chauffeur," I said.

"Call me Jilly," she reminded me, "and that new car sitting out there is half mine. And until I can drive it, you are too my personal chauffeur."

I looked at my mother. "Did you ever consider drowning her at birth?"

"Come on, Jane," my mother said. "You're going out anyway."

Jilly gave me a smug look. She walked over to Mom and gave her a hug and a kiss. "I love you, Mommy," she said.

"I love you too, honey," my mother said, going all warm and glowy.

"Oh, can I have a little extra money to get this really cute outfit I saw at the Gap?" she asked Mom innocently, as if that hadn't been the exact reason she had just hugged my mother like a drowning orphan. "It's so darling—a ruffled pink denim skirt with a matching top."

"Well, I don't know," Mom said. "You already got a three-week advance on your allowance—"

"Please-please-please-please," Jilly wheedled. "I won't ask for another thing, I swear."

"Okay," Mom finally relented, reaching for her purse. "But I'm keeping track, Jill."

"Jilly," my sister corrected her before flouncing triumphantly from the room with the cash in hand.

"You let her get away with murder," I pointed out.

"You both get away with murder," my father said, coming into the kitchen. He kissed Mom and then kissed me. "So, today's the day you go to that girl Sally's house, right?"

"Savy," I corrected him, getting up.

"Shouldn't you take something if you're invited for a meal?" my dad asked, pouring from the Mr. Coffee.

"No one does that, Dad." I went to get Jill,

who was sitting on her bed applying a second coat of mascara.

"Let's go," I told her, picking up my purse.

"I have to finish," she told me, reaching for a pink lipstick.

"Well, I'm leaving, so if you want a ride it's now or never." I studied my reflection in the mirror—medium-length brown hair, white T-shirt with Elvis Presley's picture on it, faded jeans, red high-top sneakers. It would have to do.

"I'd never go to someone's house looking like that," Jill said, rubbing her pinky over her pink lips. "I think it's tacky."

"Excuse me, but are you under the impression that someone in this room cares what you think?"

"Evidently not," she said in a cool voice, dropping her lipstick into her purse. She smoothed her sleeveless white shirt and re-creased her white shorts, then straightened the white bow in her hair. She was ready to go.

I have to admit, it felt great driving my own car, even if Jill did keep up a monologue about the cute guys at school and what they wore and which girls they liked and what these girls wore and what they were planning to wear in the future.

"Thanks," Jill said when I stopped the car in

front of the mall. "I'll call you to come and get me."

"Feel free," I told her, "but I won't be there."

"So what am I supposed to do, walk?" she demanded.

"Have one of those really cute guys from school carry you," I suggested, and sped off.

I turned the radio to the local rock oldies station and bopped along to an old Beatles tune as I followed the directions Savy had given me to her house. I admit it—I was nervous. I had no idea what to expect. What if her whole family hated me? What if I really *was* supposed to bring something?

I crossed Hillsboro Road and headed for Granny White, the street where Savy lived. I wondered briefly if the name Granny White was a leftover racist thing—like maybe the street was named after some grandmother who called her slaves "darkies" and thought she was doing them a favor if she gave them, like, a Christmas turkey to eat in their shack.

It was a beautiful street, though. The lots were huge, with old houses framed by stately trees, set far back from the street.

Finally I found Savy's address, 4500 Granny White, and turned up a long private drive. There at the top of the hill was a huge white house with white pillars and lilac shutters on the windows.

"I'm at friggin' Tara," I mumbled to myself, thinking of the plantation in *Gone With the Wind*. I parked my Sentra in the circular drive, got out, and rang the doorbell.

"Hi there!" Savy called, opening the door to usher me in. "Welcome to insanity!"

I stepped into the front hall, and I immediately knew my first impression had been incorrect.

It was bedlam.

Everywhere I looked there were signs of renovations-in-the-making. Some walls were half painted, others half plastered. A room to my right with a TV and old comfortable-looking furniture had guitar-motif wallpaper on half of one wall over red velvet–flocked paper that was peeling away. Half-built bookshelves covered one wall; empty egg crates covered another.

"Wow," I breathed.

"Yeah, tell me about it," Savy said with a laugh. "We are in the process of perpetual renovation. Gramma Beth thinks it's a good family project."

"Is it?" I asked her, stepping over a glue gun and a crusty paintbrush.

"Are you kidding?" Savy exclaimed. "We all hate it! Sometimes we humor her and start on a room, but it never lasts."

"Banzai!" a voice yelled, and seemingly out of

nowhere an electric wheelchair was heading right for me. I sidestepped it at the last minute.

"Give it a rest, Timmy," Savy called to the figure in the wheelchair. He disappeared around a corner. "Come on and meet the family," Savy said, as if Timmy and his electric wheelchair trying to run me over was perfectly normal.

We walked down a hall and down a flight of stairs. I could hear music—bluegrass—with someone taking a hot solo on a fiddle. We walked into a huge room and stood in the doorway. Savy began to clap along with the music. I looked the musicians over. An incredibly cute guy with streaky auburn hair was playing an Autoharp. Next to him an attractive, plump woman who looked just like an older version of Savy but with redder hair played the flute. A heavyset man with graying pale red hair plunked away at a stand-up bass, and a young girl with strawberry blond braids played a slide guitar. Most amazing, however, was the person playing the hot fiddle solo. She looked to be in her seventies, her skin was as white as it could be, and her hair was fire-engine red. She had on a long, colorful peasant skirt, an off-the-shoulder red blouse, and maybe twenty bangle bracelets that shook and tinkled as her bowing hand flew across the violin.

"Beep-beep!" I heard from behind me.

I feinted to one side, and the kid in the wheelchair careened into the room, full speed ahead. The little boy in the chair stopped near the couch, where he picked up some wooden spoons and began to add a rhythmic beat to the hot music. He looked over at me out of the corner of his eye, then wiggled his eyebrows.

I leaned over to Savy. "I think your little brother is flirting with me," I said in her ear.

"Yeah, Timmy's a real ladies' man, for a six-year-old!" she yelled back at me over the music.

Savy kept on clapping along with the beat, I tapped my foot, and finally they brought the number to a close. They all began whooping and hollering, congratulating themselves over how great they'd all been.

"Y'all, this is my friend Jane," Savy said. "And this is my family: Gramma Beth; my dad, Jacob; my mom, Ariel; my older brother Dustin—he's got a twin around here somewhere whose name is Dylan—my little sister, Shelaylah—call her Shelly—and my little brother who has already fallen in love with you, Timmy."

"Hi," I said softly.

"Hey" and "Welcome," they all called back at me. Timmy made kissing noises and wiggled his eyebrows some more.

"Don't mind him," Dustin said with a grin. "He's a sucker for a pretty face."

CHERIE BENNETT

I tried not to let myself grin. He had just called me pretty. And he was a world-class, to-die-for babe.

"So, how are you liking Nashville so far?" Savy's mom asked me.

"Uh, it's okay," I said noncommittally. I didn't want to tell them the truth right off, namely that I hated every square inch of Nashville and would gladly walk back to New York on hot coals if I could figure out some way to stay there once I showed up with my burnt, bleeding feet.

"It might take some getting used to, after New York," Savy's dad allowed. "But folks are real friendly here."

Yeah, sure. Not at good ole Hocum High.

"So what's this we hear about you tearing it up as a drummer?" Gramma Beth asked me, her hand on her ample hip. "Savy came home just a-gushing over you."

"I really did," Savy agreed.

"I do my best," I said modestly.

"Well, get up behind them drums, girl, and let's give a listen!" Gramma Beth cried.

"Ma, maybe Jane would like some refreshments first," Savy's dad said. "Let the poor girl catch her breath and get used to us!"

Gramma Beth made a face and rolled her eyes. "You hungry?"

"Uh, not really," I said.

42

"You thirsty?" she asked.

"Not at the moment," I said.

"Well, then, get your Yankee butt over to those drums!" she yelled, cocking her head toward a fine set by the back wall.

Everyone cracked up.

"Don't mind Gramma," Savy said, crossing to an old upright piano. "She cultivates her outrageousness. Don't you, Gramma?"

Gramma Beth ignored her. "My other grandson, Dylan, he's the drummer in the family. But lately he's been too busy composing love songs in the solitude of his room to come on down here and make music with his family. A decent hidetanning would do him a world of good, if you ask me."

Savy laughed. "Gramma, Dylan is twenty years old. I don't think you can whup him anymore."

"I can and I will," Gramma Beth assured Savy. She turned to me. "What you know how to play, girl?"

"Uh, anything," I replied.

" 'Rocky Top,' " Gramma Beth decided.

Although that was a bluegrass-country kind of tune, it was so famous that I actually knew it. "You got it," I agreed, lifting the drumsticks.

Gramma Beth counted us off, and we sailed into a rollicking version of "Rocky Top," a song about the hills of Tennessee. Gramma took a hot fiddle solo, and then Savy took a keyboard solo that sizzled. Up to that point we'd been doing instrumentals only, but then Savy leaned into the mike and started singing.

Wow, could she ever sing! Everyone else in the room picked up harmony lines, and I drummed for all I was worth. Savy brought us all home on the last soaring vocal line, the final piano riff, and we were done.

"Get out of town!" Gramma Beth hooted.

"You play some hellified drums!" Savy's dad cried.

"Thanks," I said, a big grin spreading across my face. I couldn't stop it. These people were so bizarre and enthusiastic and . . . well, kind of terrific!

We played for about an hour, doing country tunes—those I just kind of kept a beat and hung back on, since I didn't know most of them—and then rock tunes, during which I admit I really showed my stuff. Savy's whole family was really talented, but clearly the most talented ones were Savy herself and Gramma Beth.

After a while a gorgeous guy who looked just like the gorgeous guy playing the Autoharp came and stood in the doorway. Had to be Dylan. He watched me while I played.

"You've been replaced, boy!" Gramma Beth

called to him when we finished playing "Great Balls of Fire." "We got us a new drummer now!"

"You're really good," Dylan said, nodding at me.

"She's better than good," Savy's mom opined.

"Once she learns some country, she'll be pretty near unbeatable!" Shelly added.

"Well, thanks!" I said.

"You do like country, don't you?" Dustin asked me, a smile playing around his lips. Clearly he already knew the answer and was just being evil.

"Not really," I replied honestly.

"Well, then, what are you doing wearing a T-shirt with that ole country boy's picture on it?" Gramma Beth asked.

I looked down at the photo of Elvis on my T-shirt. "Elvis was the king of rock," I said.

"Ha," Gramma Beth barked. "Elvis was the king, period. King of country."

"Don't start, Gramma," Savy's dad implored his mother. He turned to me. "She always does this. She's a die-hard Elvis fan and takes it personally when someone suggests he was a rocker."

"I know what I know," Gramma Beth insisted, rubbing some rosin on her bow. She looked at her watch, then looked over at her grandson standing in the doorway. "You check on the food?"

"It's all ready," Dylan told her. "Magenta Sue just set it out on the patio."

"Let's go, then!" Savy said, getting up. "I'm starved."

"I'll lead the way!" Timmy cried, and zoomed out of the room in his electric wheelchair as if he were in an auto race. I saw him take the ramp that ran parallel to the stairs. I was very curious to know why that darling freckle-faced boy was in a wheelchair, but I figured it wasn't polite to ask. We went upstairs and walked through a bunch of rooms in various states of renovation until we got to sliding glass doors leading to a patio.

"Timmy's got JRA—juvenile rheumatoid arthritis," Savy explained as if she could read my mind. "Sometimes when it's really bad he has to use his chair. Other times he can walk."

"I never even heard of that disease," I told her.

"Most people haven't," Savy replied. "They think arthritis is something only old people get. But JRA is an autoimmune disease. Actually a lot of kids in the U.S. have it. Timmy's really feisty—well, I guess that's a Leeman character trait—and he hates it when he has to use the chair, but sometimes his joints get too painful and swollen for him to walk."

"That sucks," I said quietly, watching Timmy zoom over to the end of a huge buffet table.

"Amen," Savy said softly.

"You like country food?" Gramma Beth called over to me.

"I don't think I've ever had any," I admitted.

"It's kind of eclectic southern Jewish," Savy explained, handing me a plate and some silverware.

There was a ton of food. I helped myself to corn on the cob, greens, southern fried chicken, and coleslaw.

"That whitish lumpy stuff is Gramma's home-made gefilte fish, and the noodly casserole thing is her homemade lokshen kugel," Dustin explained. Now that both twins were together I could only tell that this one was Dustin because I remembered that he had on a blue T-shirt and Dylan had on a white T-shirt.

"Yum, I love kugel!" I exclaimed, taking a big piece.

"You know from kugel?" Gramma Beth asked me with a middle European inflection in her southern-accented voice.

I nodded. "Hey, I'm from New York. Half my friends are Jewish. I can even say the Sh'ma!"

Gramma Beth laughed. "I like this girl!" she told Savy.

"Me, too!" Savy said, giving me a grin.

We sat at a redwood table and dug into the food. It was absolutely delicious, and they all ate as if it was their last meal, then went back for more. And then more. Frankly, they ate more food than any family I'd ever seen in my life. And I kept right up with them. A pretty young girl with curly blond hair wearing cutoffs and an Opryland T-shirt began to clear off the dishes and put out dessert.

"Magenta Sue, come and meet my friend!" Savy called to her. She introduced us to each other.

"Nice to make your acquaintance," the girl said shyly in an accent so thick I could barely make out the words. She nodded at me, took my plate, and went back toward the kitchen.

"Magenta Sue helps out," Savy explained. "She lives with us."

"The only time I ever heard the name Magenta was in *The Rocky Horror Picture Show*," I said.

"Exactly!" Savy replied. "Her momma is a die-hard fan of that movie. She has two brothers, Riff and Rocky. Her family lives in Sevierville, near Dollywood."

"What's Dollywood?" I asked.

Savy looked surprised. "Wow, you really have led a sheltered life. It's Dolly Parton's amusement park in Gatlinburg. Magenta came to Nashville to try and make it as a country singer. We can go hear her one night when she's singing in a showcase club, if you want. You have room for dessert?"

I didn't, but I ate a piece of watermelon and a piece of pecan pie, anyway. "I think this is more food than I ever ate in my life," I said, feeling my stomach pressing against the snap on my jeans.

"People who don't eat a lot in this house don't get invited back," Dylan said, cutting into his pecan pie. "It's an unwritten Leeman family rule."

Magenta sat down next to me with a big piece of watermelon. "Don't pay him no never mind," she said, shaking salt on her melon. "He's a big ole teaser."

"Pit fight!" Timmy yelled, and he spit a mouthful of watermelon seeds right at me. Three stuck to my cheek.

"Timmy, that is so rude!" Savy yelled at her brother. Then she took a big bite of her watermelon and spit the pits right back at him.

After that it was a free-for-all, with the whole family and Magenta gulping down mouthfuls of melon and running after each other, spitting seeds. Gramma Beth clearly had the most experience and the best aim. Timmy would wheel right up to his target and hock those seeds right in someone's face. Everyone thought this was hilarious. After a while, I did, too. I spit out those seeds with abandon. I ran across the lawn after Dylan and got him good, right over the left side of his face. Then he picked me up—I was laughing and screaming—and he ran over to a pond near the far end of the backyard.

"Do I throw her in?" he yelled to his family.

"Nooooo!" I shrieked, kicking my legs, but I was laughing so hard I could barely get the word out.

"Do it! Do it! Do it!" Timmy chanted gleefully, buzzing across the lawn to us.

"Sorry, Jane, I always follow my little brother's orders!" Dylan told me solemnly.

He dumped me like a sack of potatoes.

I came up sputtering, water dripping off of me everywhere. All the Leemans stood there looking at me, covered in watermelon pits, happy smiles on all their faces.

Savy looked around at her family. Then she shrugged. Then she pulled her little brother out of his wheelchair.

And then without a word every single member of the Leeman family, fully clothed and covered with watermelon pits, jumped into the pond.

CHAPTER
5

♡

I couldn't describe the Leeman family to my parents. I didn't even try. I just said they were really nice and I'd had a really good time. They were satisfied with that. The truth—how absolutely, wonderfully insane they all were—I hugged to myself, smiling every time I thought about them. They were originals—exactly what I wanted to be. They definitely did *not* fit in.

Somehow getting up for school the next morning didn't seem quite so awful. I sailed through my morning classes without even caring very much that one of the pastel people pretended to gag into an imaginary barf bag when she saw my outfit, a perfectly wonderful sailor suit—the real thing from an army-navy store—with the name Rob inscribed on the pocket. Going with

51

an aquatic motif, I also wore a charm bracelet from which dangled a dozen colorful little plastic fish.

In the cafeteria I picked up a salad and a burger and looked around for Savy, but she wasn't there. I saw Kimmy Carrier, though. She was sitting by herself. She gave me a shy smile, and I walked over to her and sat down.

"Hi, where's Savy?" I asked, taking my stuff off my tray.

Kimmy shrugged. "She's late," she said in her small, shy voice. She mushed around some tuna on her plate and took a dainty, halfhearted bite. "So did you have fun at Savy's house yesterday?"

"It was a blast," I replied, biting into my burger. "Her family is outrageous!"

"They're wonderful," Kimmy said intensely.

"Oh, I meant outrageous in a good way!" I assured her. "I loved them!"

"I guess they loved you, too," Kimmy said, sounding sad.

I shrugged and watched her mush her food. Weird girl.

"Actually, Savy never invited anyone from school to play with her family before," she confided.

"No kidding?" I was surprised and flattered. "Except you, that is," I added.

"Yeah, but I could never—"

"I don't see why you take that attitude," I interrupted. "I mean, if Savy says you're good, you must be good!"

"Savy is the one and only member of my musical fan club," she said, pushing some of her long blond hair behind her ear.

"That's because she's the only one who's heard you, right?"

Kimmy nodded. "I suppose my mother kind of hears me when I play in my room at home. But she never says anything unless I'm making too much noise, and then she just tells the upstairs maid to tell me I'm giving her a headache."

"Upstairs maid?" I repeated loftily.

Kimmy blushed. "Never mind," she mumbled into her salad.

"Hey, y'all, I have big news!" Savy said, flying over to us. She sat down next to Kimmy and leaned forward, her elbows on the table. "I was just in a meeting with Ms. Jacobi and Mr. Eaton. He's the drama teacher," she added for my benefit. "Anyway, the school musical is going to be *Grease,* and they just asked me to be the musical director!"

"That's great!" Kimmy cried.

"Cool," I added, minus the enthusiasm. I shoved the last bite of burger into my mouth.

"Hey, we do really great musicals here," Savy told me, pulling a huge sandwich of beef brisket on an onion roll out of a paper bag. "We've won all kinds of awards."

"No offense, but I'm not a real musical-theater kind of babe," I told Savy. "The real musicians and the musical-theater kids at Performing Arts were in, like, two totally different worlds."

"I guess we know which one you were in," Savy said with a laugh. "How can you be from New York and hate musical theater?"

"Because it's stupid," I said. "I mean, in the middle of a conversation people break into song? And somehow they all happen to know the same dance steps?"

"It's called suspension of disbelief," Savy told me, biting into her sandwich.

"Meaning I'm supposed to leave my brain in the lobby?" I replied. "I don't think so."

Kimmy laughed. I liked her better for it.

"Ouch," Savy said. "I have a feeling this means you're not going to be up for my brilliant plan."

"Which is?" I asked.

"Well, I'll be playing keyboard, and I'm supposed to pick the musicians for the rest of the pit band. And I was hoping that both of you would do it with me."

"Count me out," Kimmy said quickly.

"Kimmy—" Savy protested.

"Savy, if I can't get up the nerve to play in

front of your family, I certainly don't have the nerve to play in front of the entire school!"

"I see your point," Savy said with a sigh, "but sometimes I just want to shake you until your teeth rattle! You are so talented, and no one knows about it!"

"Someday I'll do it," Kimmy promised.

"Oh, you've been telling me that for two years now," Savy said irritably. She turned to me. "I guess you're shooting me down, too, huh?"

"Not necessarily," I said slowly.

"You'll do it?" Savy asked, surprised.

"You're sure the musicians will be really good?" I asked her.

"Is the pope Catholic?" she replied, popping a cherry tomato in her mouth.

"Well, then . . . okay," I said. I don't know why I said yes, since the idea of spending weeks hanging out around musical-theater nerds was not my idea of a good time. Well, actually, I guess I do know why. It was because of Savy. I would have nailed my tongue to a board before I admitted how much I wanted her to like me. She was the only neon light I'd found among the pastel people.

"Cool beans!" Savy cried, reaching over to give my hand a squeeze. "Y'all, I am so psyched about this!" She glanced over at Kimmy, who looked forlorn. "Come on, Kimmy, let this be your debut. . . ."

Kimmy shook her head no. "It's not that I don't want to," she said earnestly. "I'm not being some kind of stupid prima donna. I'm just too scared."

"But if you won't do it, I'll have to ask Wyatt Shane," Savy groaned. "He's the only lead guitar player in the school good enough to handle the music. And you know how I feel about him!"

"He's in jazz band, right?" I asked. "The cute guy with the earring?"

"Yeah," Savy said. "But trust me, his beauty is skin deep."

"In other words he's a jerk," I translated.

"The biggest," Savy said. "He thinks he's God's gift to girls, and way too many girls in this school agree with him."

"I loathe guys like that," I assured her.

"Well, I'm gonna have to ask him . . ." She sighed, then gave Kimmy an imploring look.

"Don't try to make me feel guilty, Savy. You always do that," Kimmy protested.

"Look, the casting auditions are tomorrow after school," Savy told Kimmy. "Will you at least come sit in on the auditions with me and Jane before you definitely say no?"

"I'll come to the auditions with you, but I already said no," Kimmy said firmly.

Savy looked over at me. "What am I going to do with her?"

"Nothing," I replied with a shrug. "It's her life."

"But that means we have to play with Wyatt!" Savy exclaimed.

"Big deal," I scoffed. "How bad can it be?"

Savy and Kimmy looked at each other, then they both looked at me.

"Bad," they said together.

I didn't care. I wasn't afraid of some high school stud from Hocum High. So what if he was just about the cutest guy I'd ever seen in my life? I, Jane McVay, who had spent the first sixteen years of my life roaming the mean streets of New York City, not even blinking when I crossed the paths of famous movie stars, too cool to ask for an autograph when I went to the hippest clubs to hear the best musicians in the world, was immune to such superficial things.

I hoped.

"Wow, major turnout," I remarked, looking around at the eighty or so kids waiting in the school's theater to try out for *Grease* after school the next day.

"Yeah, it's always a zoo," Savy said, leading Kimmy and me to three empty seats.

"Savy, make sure you take notes on everyone," Ms. Jacobi called to Savy from the aisle. "Did you pick up the audition forms from my office?"

Savy waved a pile of forms at the teacher. "Right here," she assured her.

"Great," Ms. Jacobi said. "We'll talk after the audition, okay?"

"Don't you have to play piano for the audition?" Kimmy asked Savy.

"Nope. Barry Tucker's playing so I can listen, since I'm going to be helping teach the vocals to the singers," Savy replied.

"But all Barry Tucker can play is country!" Kimmy protested. "No one is going to audition with a country song!"

"Well, he can sight-read, sort of, if they bring music," Savy said.

"He sight-reads like a blind man," Kimmy said.

"He's a nice guy," Savy replied, looking through her forms.

"I didn't say he wasn't nice. I said he couldn't play" was Kimmy's retort.

Huh. Kimmy was actually showing some life. Evidently she took her music seriously. Pretty bizarre for someone too scared to play in private, much less in public.

"Hi," Sandra Farrell said to us as she walked by our row. "Hey, I heard you're musical director. Congrats," she added to Savy. I noticed she was looking very hip in black jeans and a red sleeveless denim shirt with black snaps.

"Thanks," Savy said. "Break a leg!"

"Right back atcha!" Sandra said with a cool smile. She continued down the aisle and signed up for the audition with the stage manager, who was seated at a table right below the stage.

"She's got a good shot at Sandy," Savy told me. "She's a really talented actress."

"She plays a mean flute, too," I added, since I'd heard her play in jazz band. "She's really good."

"Sandra Farrell is good at everything," Kimmy said with a sigh. "It's really depressing."

"She can't be good at *everything*," I objected.

"Just about," Savy said. "She's president of the junior class, gets straight A's, is captain of the varsity tennis team, and plays four instruments better than most people play one."

"And she's cute," Kimmy pointed out.

"And nice," Savy added.

I looked over at Sandra, who was thumbing through a script. "Well, I say we just off her, then. No one should be that cool and get away with it!"

Savy started numbering her audition forms. "I don't think it's so easy for her, being black at this high school. I mean, there are only maybe two dozen black kids in the whole school."

"Yeah, and they tend to hang out together," Kimmy said. "But Sandra hangs out with everybody—some people don't like her for it."

"Well, that is just ignorant," I said bluntly.

"I know," Savy agreed, sticking her red hair up in a ponytail. "But there are a lot of ignorant people in this world."

"Can I have everyone's attention, please?" Mr. Eaton called from the stage. "Everyone who is auditioning should have signed up with Kevin, our stage manager."

Kevin waved his hand at everyone.

"Most of you know the drill, but I'll go through it for new people. When Kevin calls your number, please come up and sing. If you have sheet music, give it to Barry at the piano. If you don't, just tell him what you want to sing, and he'll play it if he knows it."

"Which he never does!" a guy yelled out from the back of the theater.

"Unless it's country and has four chords in it!" someone else yelled.

Some kids laughed. "Let's hold it down to a dull roar," Mr. Eaton suggested dryly. "Now, after you sing, we may ask you to read. Scripts are available by Kevin's desk. It goes without saying that you will be polite to all the actors auditioning today and give them the respect they deserve. Thank you."

"It'll take forever to get through this mob," I said. The crowd was now up to around one hundred kids.

"Most of them will just sing part of a song and then you'll hear a loud 'thank-you' from Mr. Eaton or Ms. Jacobi," Savy assured me. "Besides, some of the kids are just here to watch."

One by one the auditioners went up onstage. Barry Tucker was not the world's greatest accompanist, but then none of the kids were the world's greatest singer. In fact, most of them couldn't sing if their lives depended on it. Most of the auditioners tried to struggle through a song from *Grease*—my idea of torture is sitting through "Worse Things," Rizzo's big ballad, sung badly for two hours. Barry couldn't play it at all, even though the score to the show was sitting right in front of him. After hearing the first fifteen singers, I was ready to jump ship—I can handle only so much bad singing—but then a girl with pale skin, curly black hair, and a kind of horsey overbite came on stage and went to talk with Barry.

"That's Judy Gillette," Savy whispered to me. "She's great."

"Compared to what's been up there, Milli Vanilli is great," I whispered back to her.

"Wait, you'll see," Savy said, writing Judy's name on the top of an audition form.

I watched Judy talking with Barry. He nodded

at whatever it was she said. She walked to center stage, and Barry began to confidently play an introduction on the piano. There was no music in front of him.

Savy leaned over to me. "Smart. She's going to sing 'Crazy,' a tune Barry actually knows. It's a country standard by—"

"Patsy Cline," I interrupted. "I'm not *that* ignorant."

Savy smiled at me. "I thought you didn't know country."

"I don't," I replied. "But everyone who's anyone knows Patsy Cline."

I listened to Judy sing. She was really good—strong, confident, controlled. In fact, she sounded a lot like a young Patsy Cline, which probably just meant that she hadn't developed her own style yet. She finished with a major vocal riff. The kids in the audience applauded and whistled enthusiastically.

"I would give my right arm to have that kind of confidence," Kimmy said wistfully.

"Number fifty-eight!" Kevin called. A darling guy with black hair jumped up on stage instead of using the stairs.

"Who's that?" I asked Savy.

"Sawyer Paxton," Savy replied. "He's a senior. Doesn't he look familiar to you?"

I watched Sawyer talking with Barry. He was

wearing a royal blue T-shirt and faded jeans. He really was cute. "Should he?" I asked Savy.

"He looks just like his father," Kimmy said, her eyes glued to Sawyer. She turned to me. "Doesn't the name Judd Paxton mean anything to you?"

"No," I replied.

"His daddy is only the top country songwriter of all time," Kimmy replied, as if I were from another planet.

I stared blankly at Kimmy.

" 'Until Love Fades'? 'Memories of Mary'? 'The Last Rose of Summer'?" she asked me.

"Isn't 'Until Love Fades' a jazz standard?" I asked.

"It was a country standard first," Kimmy explained loftily. "Judd Paxton is in the Country Music Hall of Fame. He's written more number-one songs than anyone in history."

"So, does his kid have any talent?"

"You tell us," Savy said, as Sawyer walked to center stage.

Yowza. The guy was great. I mean really, really great. He was singing "Worse Things," but he was singing it a cappella—meaning without accompaniment. Evidently what he'd been saying to Barry was "Don't play." Wise choice.

"Now, *he* is really *good*," I said to Savy.

I looked over at Kimmy. She was leaning forward in her seat, breathing in synchronization with Sawyer Paxton as he sang "Worse Things." She had taken off her glasses. Her eyes were two huge blue Frisbees of love.

"Did you ever go out with him?" I asked Kimmy.

She blushed furiously and ducked her long neck so far down that her chin receded into the neckline of her shirt. "Of course not," she whispered. "He doesn't even know I'm alive."

"Maybe if he heard you play the guitar he'd notice you," Savy suggested.

"Shhh, I want to hear him finish," Kimmy hissed. She clasped her hands in her lap and mooned over Sawyer as he hit the final soaring notes of the song.

"That ole lust-bunny has just jumped in Kimmy's drawers," Savy drawled.

I laughed. "I don't blame her," I admitted. "Talent is sexy."

"So's his butt," Savy whispered to me.

I cracked up as everyone in the room applauded and hooted for Sawyer. He walked up the aisle, heading for the rear door of the theater.

"Now's your chance, Kimmy," Savy teased her friend. "Just reach over and grab him, tell him you have to have him or die!"

Kimmy poked Savy hard in the ribs and sank down lower in her seat.

But then, as if Kimmy had wished it, Sawyer walked up the aisle and stopped right in front of us.

"Hey, could I talk to you for a minute?" Sawyer said.

Savy and I both looked over at Kimmy.

"He's talking to you," Kimmy told me in a low voice.

I turned to look at Sawyer. "Me?"

He nodded.

"Uh, yeah, I guess," I said.

I walked out of the theater with Sawyer, feeling Savy's curiosity and Kimmy's envy follow me out the door.

CHAPTER
6

That night I was lying on my bed reading "The Metamorphosis" for World Lit—my teacher adored it and had assigned it specially—my Walkman in place, Arrested Development rapping into my earphones, when dear, sweet "Jilly" flounced into our room and pulled the earphones from my ears.

"I know there's a really good reason you did that, which I'm going to listen to before I kill you," I told her. I kept my finger at page twenty-seven of the long story to keep my place.

"I have a problem," she said, sitting on her bed.

"Good for you, something of your very own." I put the earphones back on.

"I am serious!" she yelled.

I took off the earphones and put them around my neck. "Well?" I asked her impatiently.

"There's this guy I really like—Billy Bob," she began.

"No one is named Billy Bob," I told her. "That's one of those made-up names from southern prison movies."

"Billy Bob Kilroy," she continued pointedly. "He's just the coolest thing in my entire school."

"Can we cut to the chase here?"

"Well, Billy Bob likes me. I know he does. Everyone says so," Jill continued, nervously twisting her charm bracelet around and around her wrist. "There's this dance coming up at school with a *Gone With the Wind* theme, and I really want him to invite me."

"Uh-huh . . ."

"But he hasn't," Jill finished.

"So invite him," I suggested.

"Jane, that is so lame! I could never!"

"Okay, don't," I said, reaching for my earphones.

"I'm not done," Jill said quickly. "Billy Bob has an older sister, Katie Lynn—"

"Does everyone in their family have two names?" I asked. "Aren't we talking major cliché here?"

"Katie Lynn Kilroy?" Jill repeated. "Doesn't that ring a bell?"

I started to shake my head no, but then a vision of one of the more odious of the pastel people swam into my mind—a perky little blond-haired cheerleader who laughed and pointed at me each and every day. In fact, she was the first one I had overheard call me "that weird girl from New York." What a charmer.

"Jill, you're better off without ole Billy Bob," I told her. "I think mental illness runs in his family."

"If you would stop making jokes, I could tell you my problem," Jill said earnestly. "Katie Lynn told Billy Bob all about you, how you wear these geeky outfits and have six holes pierced in one of your ears but not the other one, and how you walk around like yours doesn't stink—and Billy Bob told me."

"And you like this moron?" I asked. I felt hurt but refused to show it.

"Jane, we don't live in New York anymore!" Jill cried. "Can't you stop acting like such a weirdo?"

"Jill, the pastel people have invaded your mind. There may be surgery we can perform. It may not be too late—"

"Stop it! Just stop it!" Jill yelled, jumping up from her bed. "You think it's so cute and original, the stuff you wear? A nurse's uniform? A hula skirt? And that thing you wore today—a leopard-print skirt and a T-shirt that says 'Endangered Species Furriers'?"

"It was a joke," I protested.

"Well, it isn't funny!" Jill yelled. "It's totally humiliating! Kids are laughing at me just because you're my sister! Billy Bob won't even ask me out!"

"Your family loyalty is touching," I said with a sour smile.

Jill came over and sat next to me. "I really, really want to fit in here," she told me earnestly. "I like it here, and I just want the other kids to like me."

She looked so sweet and vulnerable there that for a moment I remembered my little sister, Jill, as she'd been back in New York. Sure, she'd been a suck-up even then, but she'd had her occasional moments of lucidity. I loved her. I put my arm around her.

"And they're never going to like me as long as my sister is a freak," she concluded.

I moved my arm.

"Gee, Jill," I said, "much as I'd like to have a lobotomy just so you could get a date, I'm gonna be forced to pass on this one." I lay down on the bed and opened my book to "The Metamorphosis."

"Okay, fine, I should have known you didn't give a rat's ass about me," Jill cried as she ran to the door. "Mommy!" I heard her yell on her way down the hall.

"I can't believe we come from the same gene pool," I muttered, settling down with my book. Just as Gregor Samsa was turning into a huge insect, the phone rang by my bed.

"Hello?"

"Hey, it's Savy."

"Hi. Hey, did you read 'The Metamorphosis'?" I asked her.

"Sure," she replied. "It's a great story."

"So what happens after page twenty-seven?" I asked her.

"Read it and find out!" she replied good-naturedly. "Listen, it's major cool about Sawyer Paxton," she added.

I smiled into the phone. It really was kind of cool. When Sawyer asked to speak to me that afternoon, he told me he'd heard from his friend Wyatt Shane that I was a really great drummer, and his drummer had mono, and would I like to fill in on a session the following week for a demo he was doing?

The good news was I knew the guy had a great voice. The bad news was it was a country demo. I ignored the bad part and said yes. My very first demo session. Major psych.

"I'm surprised Wyatt Shane even knew my name to recommend me to Sawyer," I told Savy.

"Well, that's kind of why I called you," Savy said. "I just got off the phone with Wyatt. I asked him to play in the pit band for *Grease*. He said no way was he playing guitar for some lame high school musical."

"So, big deal, we'll find someone else," I told Savy.

"All the guitarists in this school besides Kimmy and Wyatt are second rate," Savy replied. "Do you want a second-rate player?"

"Let's fly my boyfriend, Chad, in from New York," I suggested. "He's killer."

"Our budget won't stretch that far," Savy said with a sigh.

"So let's bag it, then. It'll be torture if the musicians aren't any good."

"Oy, McVay," Savy groaned into the phone. "That's your idea of a solution?"

I laughed. My former best friend from when I still had a life, Anita Lebowitz, had picked up the expression "oy vay" from her grandmother. Now Savy was using the same Yiddish word.

"Maybe I should change my name to Oy McVay," I mused. "It has a certain ring to it. Kinda punk, don't you think?"

"Jane, you are as useless as a one-legged man in a butt-kicking contest," Savy drawled. I noticed her drawl got thicker when she was irritated.

"Okay, I'll try to be more useful," I replied solemnly. "What do we do?"

"Not 'we,' you," Savy said firmly. "When I told Wyatt you were playing drums for the show he almost seemed tempted. He went on and on about what a great drummer you are."

"No sugar?" I asked.

"No sugar," Savy confirmed. "So I was thinking, maybe tomorrow at school you could ask Wyatt yourself if he'll play for the show. Maybe you'll have better luck than I did."

"Hey, he doesn't even know me!" I protested. The very idea of asking him made me nervous, but I would never admit it. "He's not about to say yes to me after he turned you down."

"He might!" Savy said. "He thinks you're this incredibly hip, cool drummer from New York—"

"Well, I am, but—"

"So good, then, you'll ask him," Savy concluded. "You're not scared, are you?"

"Of Wyatt Shane?" I scoffed. "Give me a break!"

"Great then, ask him in band tomorrow," Savy said. "I gotta run and pretend to paint one of the walls in the bathroom before Gramma Beth has a coronary. See ya!"

I rolled over onto my back and stared at the ceiling. Tomorrow I had to ask Wyatt Shane to play in the pit band for the high school play. So?

No biggie. He'd say no and that would be that. But if he said no, the band would suck, and I would be forced to play with some amateur fool and the whole thing would sound like major dogmeat.

There was only one solution: I had to think of some way to get Wyatt Shane to say yes.

The next day I dressed carefully in vintage grunge: ancient jeans, a tie-died T-shirt, and a white macramé vest. Dangling from a cord around my neck was a giant peace symbol. Around my forehead I wore a love bead headband. I surveyed the results in the mirror: fabulous. I could have been at Woodstock.

Jill snorted her oatmeal when I came to breakfast.

"You see what I mean, Mom?" she whined. "She only dresses like that to embarrass me!"

"I happen to look great," I told her, flipping her a peace sign. I poured myself a glass of juice.

"You look like a freak!" Jill cried.

I surveyed her outfit du jour: a peach-colored split skirt with a matching pink- and peach-toned ruffled blouse. Her hair bow was peach, too, natch. "So, you are suggesting that I should dress like you, right?" I asked her.

"Right," Jilly replied.

"You didn't used to dress like that," I pointed out. "You're the one who changed, not me."

"God, don't you know anything?" Jilly cried. "This is how kids dress here!"

"It kind of makes me want to hurl," I said conversationally, pouring myself a bowl of cereal. "You look like a walking fruit stand."

"Mom!" Jill whined.

"Please, girls, give me a break," my mother pleaded, sipping her coffee.

"Wow, we're late," I said, looking at my watch. "We gotta boogie." I got up quickly and grabbed my books. I kissed my mom on the cheek and sang "The Age of Aquarius" as loud as I could walking out to the car. The lady in the next apartment gave me a funny look, and I flipped her a peace sign. Jill slunk out behind me muttering something under her breath about wanting to die.

I dropped Jill off and headed over to Hocum High. I figured I'd have all morning to figure out the best approach with Wyatt, but just as I was walking into school there he was, just coming out of Ms. Jacobi's office. He had on faded jeans and a denim work shirt with the sleeves rolled up. I noticed how tan his arms were, covered with golden blond hairs. The same color as the golden streaks in his long hair.

"Hi," Wyatt said easily, falling into step with me.

"Oh, hi," I said casually.

"Cool outfit," he told me, giving me an appreciative look.

"Thanks."

"So, I hear you're gonna play on Sawyer's demo next week," Wyatt said.

"Yeah," I replied. "Is his tune any good?"

"I haven't heard it," Wyatt admitted. "But he's a great singer."

"Yeah, I heard his audition for the school play," I told him.

Wyatt stopped walking and looked at me, cocking his head to one side. "Hey, are you really playing in the pit band for that school thing? That's what Savy told me."

"Yeah, I am."

"Why?" Wyatt asked me curiously, shaking some of his perfectly streaked hair out of his face.

"Because Savy's a really good musician and because she's my friend," I answered honestly.

"She's good," Wyatt allowed, "but a school play?"

"So?" I challenged him. "Good music is wherever you make it."

Wyatt gave me a skeptical look. "Savy asked me to play lead for that thing. I told her no way."

"I think you should do it," I said casually, leaning against a locker.

"Oh, yeah?" Wyatt asked. Slowly he put his

hand on the wall over my head and leaned in to me. "How come?"

I could smell his toothpaste and something deliciously musky, like patchouli oil. The little hairs on the back of my neck tingled. *You are in love with Chad,* I reminded myself. "Because you're a good player, and if you play lead we'll have a good pit band," I said simply.

"You want me to do it?" he asked me in a low voice, leaning in even closer to me

"Yeah," I squeaked, then cleared my throat. "I mean, sure, if you want to," I added as casually as I could.

"So what will you do for me in return?" he asked me, a lazy, insinuating smile playing at the corners of his mouth.

"Drum so good that you'll sound decent for a change," I replied, giving him a bored look.

Wyatt laughed. "Ooh, aren't you the cool one."

"Yeah, I'm also the late one," I said, ducking under his arm. I took a few steps away from him and then turned around to walk backward. "So I'll tell Savy you're in, right?"

"If you say so, tough girl," he drawled, giving me a mock salute.

"Cool," I replied, then spun around and hurried down the hall.

Woah, baby. Wyatt had definitely been flirting with me. And I had definitely liked it.

"Jane!" Savy ran up to me from the science wing. "I've got great news!"

"Me too!" I replied.

"Wyatt said he'd play in the band!" we both said at the same time.

"Hold on," I told her. "I just had this conversation with him, back there," I pointed behind me. "What did you do, fly into the science wing?"

"No, I just ran into Ms. Jacobi, and she told me she promised him extra music credit," Savy explained. "He's not gonna have to do the term paper the rest of us have to do on a famous composer."

"Oh." I couldn't think of anything else to say.

"Didn't he tell you that?" Savy asked me.

"Not exactly," I said slowly.

"What did he do, tell you he was only doing it for you and flirt with you outrageously like the low-life, lying scum bucket that he is?"

"Uh, no, nothing like that—"

"Well, I wouldn't put it past him," Savy interrupted. "I'm glad he's gonna be in the band, because frankly we need him, but I'd watch out for him if I were you."

"Savy, no offense, but some Hocum High Romeo who thinks he's a super stud is not my idea of exciting," I coolly informed her.

"Good," Savy said approvingly. "I mean, he is seriously bad news. He's really wild—drugs, drinking, all that. He got arrested for drunk driving last year. And rumor has it his girlfriend from Hillsboro High got pregnant and then left town."

"How do you know all that stuff is true?" I asked Savy.

"Come on!" Savy chided me. "Everyone knows everything that happens in this school!"

"I just don't want to prejudge the guy," I said. "Besides, Kimmy likes him," I reminded her.

"Kimmy is the last completely innocent girl at Green Hills High," Savy intoned meaningfully. She cocked her head at me. "You didn't fall for his line of b.s., did you?"

"Never happen," I said firmly.

"Good," Savy replied. "Because just about every other girl at this school did."

"Did you?" I asked her pointedly.

"No," Savy said.

"Did he ask?"

"No," she admitted.

"Would you if he did?"

Savy actually blushed. "Of course not," she finally managed. "His ego is bigger than his IQ."

I laughed, just as the bell rang for first period.

"Gotta motor, catch ya later," I told her, hurrying off in the other direction.

So Wyatt had already known he was going to

be in the band when he'd caught up with me coming into school. Which meant he just wanted to flirt with me. Which is exactly what Savy had just warned me about. Good thing.

So why did I feel all fluttery inside just thinking about seeing him again?

There was only one explanation: the pastel people really *had* invaded my brain.

CHAPTER 7

♡

And so how is it that Kafka's 'The Metamorphosis' is, in fact, an allegory relevant to every person's life?" My Lit teacher, Mr. Gerksky, a toady-looking little man with protruding eyeballs and yellowish skin, stared out expectantly at the class.

It was the next day. I sank down lower in my seat. I had somehow neglected to finish reading the story. I got as far as figuring out that some guy named Gregor actually turned into an insect. This was not my idea of riveting reading. Besides, I'd been watching MTV while I read the story, and this great new tune had come on, and I had to stop to listen, and then I had to try to work out a drum solo for it.

"Jane?" Mr. Gerksky asked expectantly.

Oh, of course he had to call on me. Teachers have some kind of radar—they zero right in on you when you haven't done your homework. There is nothing a high school teacher loves more than humiliating his or her students. I felt color flooding my face.

"Uh, well, it's really relevant," I mumbled.

"Because?" Mr. Gerksky prompted, his buggy little eyes boring into mine.

"Because, uh, things can change like they changed for ... um ... Gregor," I tried, desperately stalling for time. I snuck a glance at the clock. There were forty-five minutes left before the class ended.

No way out. No way out.

"Changed how?" the teacher asked me drolly.

"Well, like, the guy changed into a bug," I pointed out.

Laughter. Mr. Gerksky looked sharply around the room, then back at me.

"Ms. McVay, did you read this story?"

"Some of it," I replied, wishing I could fall through a hole in the floor. Everyone was staring at me.

" 'Some of it' does not allow you to enter into an intelligent conversation about the story, does it?"

"Y'all, she must have been too busy shopping

for that outfit she has on!" Katie Lynn Kilroy hissed from behind me.

A bunch of people laughed. I happened to have on a great outfit—an oversized jumper with high lace-up ankle boots. I had attached a fake braid at the back of my head. I call it my "Little House on the Prairie" look—very Laura Ingalls Wilder. I whipped around and gave Katie the evil eye. She rolled her eyes and stuck her finger down her throat, pretending to gag.

"Well, Jane, perhaps you'll do me the honor of reading the rest of Mr. Kafka's classic this evening," Mr. Gerksky intoned.

"Sure," I agreed.

"Splendid. And tomorrow you'll bring in a five-page paper dealing with the subject of allegory in 'The Metamorphosis,' won't you?"

"I have a feeling that wasn't a multiple choice question," I muttered.

"Your feeling is correct," Mr. Gerksky replied smugly. "Now, for those of you interested in actually *passing* this course, let's discuss Kafka's story. Perhaps Ms. McVay will learn something."

Gee, what a charming guy. He sure inspired me to read that story. Sha, right. How the hell was I supposed to read the story and write a five-page paper on the stupid thing by the next day when the very first practice for the pit band was scheduled for that night at seven? I didn't even get home from school until three-thirty! Maybe I could find some Cliff Notes or something. . . .

The bell finally rang, and I headed for the door. I saw Savy and Kimmy headed for chemistry.

"Hey there!" Savy called to me, her usual upbeat self. Then she saw my face. "What happened?"

"Gerksky just ragged me out in front of the whole class," I told her. "I've got to write a paper tonight about 'The Metamorphosis.'"

"Oh, I really liked that story," Kimmy said in her soft voice, hugging her books to her slender chest.

"Can you tell me what it's about in the next two minutes?" I asked her hopefully.

"Well, it's complicated," she began.

"Can't you uncomplicate it?" I asked her. "I've got band practice tonight at seven. I'll never be able to read the story and write the paper this afternoon!"

Kimmy's face fell. "Right. Band practice." She looked forlornly at Savy.

"Don't give me cow eyes, Kimmy!" Savy protested. "You could have been in the band, but you didn't want to."

"I know," Kimmy agreed with a sigh. She stared at the floor looking utterly miserable.

"Can we go back to 'The Metamorphosis'?" I suggested. "What's the big allegory in it?"

Both girls ignored me. "Look, you can still change your mind," Savy told Kimmy. "I'll be more than happy to get rid of Wyatt."

"You know I can't!" Kimmy exclaimed.

"I know you *won't*," Savy corrected, her southern accent becoming more pronounced as her temper flared.

"Uh, hel-lo, about that story . . ." I reminded them.

They continued down the hall, arguing all the way. I watched them go and sighed loudly. So much for a little help from my friends. I was just going to have to speed-read and write the world's fastest paper.

It was after school, and I lay on my bed trying to speed-read "The Metamorphosis." My eye kept hitting on the clock—4:15, and I still had lots of pages left to cover. I forced my eye back to the page, taking in a few more lines. It was sooooo boring.

"Who decided this thing was a classic? That's what I want to know," I mumbled out loud. I looked at the clock again—4:18.

I heard the doorbell ring. It had to be either one of our chatty neighbors—the one next door baked us butterscotch chip cookies and tried to sell us Tupperware—or one of Jilly's new bosom buddies. I forced myself to read.

Knock-knock-knock on my bedroom door.

"Jane, someone is here for you," my mom called through the door.

"For me?" I asked, completely perplexed.

My mother stuck her head in. "Tall, blond, very pretty, says her name is Kimmy," my mom said eagerly, like it was some kind of big wow that I had made a friend who would actually come over to our cruddy little apartment.

"Kimmy Carrier?" I asked with surprise.

My mother shrugged. "She seems terribly nervous."

"Oh, she's always like that," I said, and went down the hall to find Kimmy sitting in our minuscule living room. She was perched on the edge of the couch as if she were waiting for a countdown to launch herself into space.

"Hi!" she called, jumping up the instant she saw me.

"Hi," I replied, taking a seat near her. "So . . . what brings you here?"

"I know you didn't invite me," Kimmy whispered anxiously. She sat back down.

"Hey, it's fine," I assured her. "I'm just . . . uh . . . surprised to see you, I guess."

"I know," Kimmy agreed. She looked around our apartment. "Nice place," she said politely. I've noticed that everyone in the South is nauseatingly polite—to your face, that is.

"No, it isn't," I said bluntly. "We're building a house in Greenhills Estates subdivision, that's why we're here."

"Oh, well, it's nice there," Kimmy said lamely.

"No, it's hideous," I told her. "All the houses look the same. They cut down all the trees and planted little tiny trees in their place. Does that make any sense to you?"

"I guess not," Kimmy agreed.

We stared at each other.

"Well, cool, we've covered architecture pretty thoroughly," I finally said.

Kimmy gave me a sickly little smile.

Silence.

"Did you want a drink or something?" I finally asked her.

"Oh, no, thanks for offering," she said politely.

Silence.

"Gee, I really have to finish that story—you know, the one I have to write a paper on in the next two hours?" I reminded her.

"I know," she said. "That's kind of why I came by." She reached into a binder that she'd been clutching and pulled out a few sheets of paper stapled together. "This is a paper I wrote on 'The Metamorphosis' last year. I mean, I thought it might help you." She held it out to me.

I took the paper. "The Metamorphosis of the Human Spirit," the cover read. Next to that was marked a large *A* and a handwritten comment, "Excellent work as always."

"I didn't mean you should copy it or anything," she rushed on. "I just thought that maybe it would help you, give you some ideas or something." She pushed her glasses up her nose and bit at the inside of her lower lip.

"Wow, this is really nice of you," I told her. And I meant it.

"Oh, it's nothing," she assured me.

Beep, beep, beep!

I stared at Kimmy's purse, which was where the sound was coming from.

"You carry a beeper?" I asked her with surprise.

"Oh, you know," she said evasively, jumping up from the couch and edging toward the front door. "So, have fun at band practice tonight and everything."

"Sure," I said.

"Tell Savy ... I mean, I wish I could ... Tell her not to be mad at me."

"She's not mad at you," I told Kimmy. "You're her best friend."

Kimmy looked at me sorrowfully, her blue eyes magnified behind her glasses. "Not anymore," she blurted out, then she ran out the door.

Extremely weird girl. Nice. But extremely weird.

*   *   *

I showed up at Savy's for band practice right on time. Okay, I admit it—I was psyched, both about playing and about seeing Wyatt. I told myself I shouldn't be, but I couldn't help it. Maybe all those rumors about him weren't true. Maybe he just really liked me. Sue me, I've got a great weakness for musicians.

"Hey, glad to see you!" Savy said, giving me a hug at her front door. She had just seen me a few hours earlier at school. She was the most genuinely enthusiastic person I had ever met. She was looking very cute in wide-legged painter's pants with huge Mickey Mouses all over them, and an oversized T-shirt that read "Mickey has it tough: he's short, he's black, and he's a mouse." I wore my favorite jeans with a zillion holes in them and a High School of Performing Arts sweatshirt. Cazh but cool, I figured.

"Wyatt's not here yet, but Sandra is," Savy said, leading the way to the music room. "I bribed Timmy to stay in his room with some homemade cookies or he'd be out here mooning all over you," she added.

"What's Sandra play besides flute?" I asked as we headed for the music room.

"Bass, guitar, and piano," Savy replied, "but in the pit band she'll be covering bass and flute."

"I'm surprised she didn't get the part of Sandy," I told Savy.

"I'm not," Sandra said, evidently overhearing my comment as we walked into the music room. "Judy Gillette has a better voice than I do."

Sandra was sitting at the old upright piano noo-dling some riffs up and down the keyboard. She had on khaki shorts and a plain white T-shirt. I could see what great shape she was in—muscular and toned. Clearly she worked out hard. She also looked perfectly groomed, and had every time I'd ever seen her. I always wonder how people like that get through a day without a loose thread, a hangnail, a zit, or a split end. A pact with the devil is one possibility.

"You don't sound very upset," I said, sitting on an old aqua couch half covered with new floral chintz.

Sandra shrugged and hit another chord on the piano. "I don't have any great aspirations to be an actress. Judy does."

"You've got a great attitude," I commented, dropping my jean jacket on the couch.

Sandra shrugged again. "Life is too short to sweat the little stuff." She looked at her watch. "Wyatt's late."

"What else is new?" Savy said, rolling her eyes.

"It's a pattern," Sandra told me. "Wyatt be-lieves the whole world should be delighted to await his presence."

"What is it with this guy?" I asked them. "I

mean, what makes him think he's God's gift to the universe?"

"The five hundred girls who have told him so, I would imagine," Savy said dryly. She took two scores to *Grease* off the top of the piano and handed one to Sandra and one to me.

"Let's go through some stuff without him," Savy suggested.

"Okay," Sandra agreed. "Darryl is coming over at nine-thirty, so I've got to leave here by nine."

"Her boyfriend," Savy explained. "He graduated from Green Hills two years ago, and now he goes to Fisk. He's going to be a doctor. We're talking major brain."

"Well, he's cute, too," Sandra added with a grin, thumbing through her score.

"Yeah, the two of you are going to be the two cutest doctors in Tennessee," Savy told Sandra, writing something in the margin of her music.

"You want to be a doctor?" I asked Sandra.

"I'm *going* to be a doctor," she corrected me.

"You kill me," Savy told Sandra with a sigh. "I don't know what I want to do next week, much less with the rest of my life. Do you, Jane?"

"Sure," I replied easily. "I want a recording deal with a major label, I want to play drums on tour with Michael Jackson, and I want to be Christian Slater's love slave."

90

Sandra laughed. "How about Christian Slater being *your* love slave?"

"I like the way your mind works," I said, nodding in agreement.

"There's only one thing I've always wanted," Savy said wistfully, pulling her legs up Indianfashion on the piano bench. "I've always wanted my own band."

"So start a band," I told her. "That's what my boyfriend Chad and I did in New York."

"I want my own *country* band," Savy added.

I winced. "That stuff is a sorry excuse for music."

"Not all of it," Sandra put in. She pulled her bass guitar out of the case.

I was surprised. "You listen to country?"

"I listen to what's good," Sandra said, sliding her guitar strap over her shoulder. "Some of this, some of that."

"You don't think country music is . . . well, racist?" I asked her.

Sandra smiled. "Hey, it's just white boy's blues," she explained. "And good blues is good blues. Period. It's only racist if it's played by racists."

I gave her a dubious look. Personally I was not convinced. As far as I was concerned, country music and the South were racist by definition. Not that I'd seen any more overt racism in Nashville than I'd seen in New York, but hey, history is history.

Savy turned to the middle of her music score and pressed the pages open on the piano stand. "Let's skip the overture. It'll fall into place once we've learned the tunes, anyway," Savy suggested. "Want to start with 'We Go Together,' since we all know it?"

The doorbell chimed.

"And speaking of 'We Go Together,' Sandra murmured, "I think His Bodaciousness just rang."

"Be right back," Savy said, and ran to get the door.

I busied myself with some drum riffs until Savy came back into the room with Wyatt. I was sure my nervousness about him didn't show on my face, but I could feel Sandra looking at me contemplatively.

"Hi," Wyatt said when he came into the room. He was wearing an old black leather jacket with a peace symbol painted on the back, jeans, and a flannel shirt. His streaky blondish-brownish hair was clean and loose, flowing over his shoulders. When he pushed his hair back with a careless gesture I could see the diamond stud glinting in his ear.

"Can we just get started?" Sandra asked him irritably. "You kept all of us waiting."

"Chill out, Sandra," Wyatt told her, taking his guitar out of its case. "No one is grading you on this."

"That is not the point," Sandra snapped. "You are incredibly inconsiderate."

Wyatt walked slowly over to Sandra and gave her a lazy, confident grin. "Don't you ever just kick back with a brew and say 'I'm off duty'?"

"No, I don't 'kick back with a brew' because I don't drink," Sandra said, overemphasizing every word.

"Too bad," Wyatt murmured. "It might loosen you up."

"Uh, look, I don't think we're off to a great start here," Savy interrupted. "Let's just get into the music, okay?"

"Fine," Sandra said coolly.

"Let's rock 'n' roll," Wyatt agreed.

Savy gave him a score, which he set up on the music stand in front of him. We started with "We Go Together," which sounded pretty good the very first time through. By the third time we played it, it sounded great. After that we went through three more of the songs from the show, which were more difficult. Sandra and Savy were better sight readers than Wyatt, I noted.

Just when we finished playing "Mooning,"

Gramma Beth stuck her head into the music room.

"Y'all ready for a break?" she asked us.

"Sure," Savy agreed. "We can take ten."

"Good," Gramma Beth said, carrying in a huge tray of food, "because I need some young'uns to dig into these desserts."

Savy introduced Sandra and Wyatt to her grandmother. Gramma Beth gave me a big hug, and I, normally not a real huggy kind of person, hugged her right back. In my book Gramma Beth is the coolest thing walking.

"Try the chess pie," she urged me.

"What is it?" I asked, staring at the pale custardy-looking dessert.

"It's sugar, eggs, butter, vanilla ... in a pie-crust," Gramma Beth replied. I looked at her blankly, and she laughed. "Shoot, you really are a Yankee, girl! It's chess pie!"

I tried a slice. It was actually really good. I had polished off the pie and was on my second chocolate chip cookie when Wyatt came over and sat next to me on the couch.

"Can you believe this lame music?" he asked me.

"It's not so bad," I replied, swallowing the last of the cookie.

"What, it speaks to you?" Wyatt wondered.

"Not really," I replied honestly.

Wyatt leaned close to me and looked me dead in the eye. "So what speaks to you?"

I glanced quickly across the room. Savy had helped her grandmother carry out some dishes. Sandra had her head buried in a book. "You mean, like, musically?" I asked him, trying to sound nonchalant.

Wyatt laughed a low laugh. "No, I mean what speaks to you at all. What makes you hot?" He stared at my lips.

"If this is, like, some kind of Tennessee-boy come-on, I am truly bored," I replied laconically.

Wyatt smiled, clearly not in the least disturbed. "You have some chocolate on your mouth," he said in a low voice.

"Where?" I asked. I lifted my hand to wipe off the chocolate. Wyatt caught my hand in his. Then with his other hand he slowly and gently wiped the corner of my mouth with one knuckle.

"So, Jane McVay," Wyatt said, "you want to hear some real music sometime?"

"So, Wyatt Shane," I said back to him, "I listen to real music all the time. I'm from New York, where we actually know what real music is."

"Yeah, I know, tough girl," he teased me. "You've been everywhere and you've done everything, right?"

"Right," I agreed, staring him dead in the eye.

No way was this southern-fried stud muffin getting the best of Jane McVay. No way.

"You know people think I'm bad, don't you?" he asked me.

"Rumor has it," I replied. Then I yawned in his face.

He laughed. "Yeah, you're as bad as I am. I can tell. Listen, why don't you come hear my band, Thunder Rolls, play at this party a week from Saturday? We can hang out." He took a slip of paper out of the pocket of his jeans and handed it to me. An address was written on it.

"A week from Saturday?" I asked him in a mocking voice. "You country boys sure do plan ahead."

"When we want something, we do," he agreed with a grin.

"So why would I want to come to this party?" I asked him.

"Because my band is killer," he told me. Then he leaned even closer. "And because you're wondering what it's going to be like when I kiss you."

"Y'all ready to get back to it?" Savy called, coming back into the room.

Wyatt gave me a final slow look, then stood up and walked that sexy, lanky walk of his back over to his guitar.

I stuffed the piece of paper into the pocket of my jeans. I saw the warning look Savy gave me, but I ignored it. So what if I just went to hear his band play? It didn't have to be such a big deal. It didn't have to be a date or anything.

I went back behind the drums, and we went over the intro music to Act Two, but all the time I was playing I was seeing me and Wyatt at that party.

And I was wondering what it would be like when he kissed me.

CHAPTER
8

ꔷ

*B*etween school, pit band practice, and homework the next two weeks passed really quickly. Our pit band started getting hot—there actually *were* good musicians in Nashville, after all.

Okay, I know you're wondering what I did about the party Wyatt had invited me to. I turned him down. Not because I didn't want to go, because I did. But Savy, by far my favorite person at Hocum High, warned me again and again that Wyatt was a jerk. I felt her watching us whenever Wyatt flirted with me at band practice.

We moved our band rehearsals to school for the last week of practice, so we could play during the run-throughs. Judy Gillette was great as Sandy, and Sawyer Paxton was incredible as Danny. Sometimes I'd notice Kimmy sitting in the back of the theater, just staring at Sawyer, with this hangdog look on her face. Once he tried to talk to her, and she actually ran out of the theater. When Savy and Sandra and I would try to get her to go out with us after band practice, she always said she didn't want to intrude. What do you do with someone like that? The girl didn't even know how great looking she was—or could be, if she'd maybe stop hunching over, lose her glasses, and get a life.

During our final full week of rehearsals for the play, Wyatt invited me to another party. It was the same come-on: he handed me a piece of paper with an address and told me the party was Sunday night. By this time I was dreaming about him. I just couldn't help myself. I didn't admit this to anyone, of course. I barely even admitted it to myself. But then two things happened on Friday that put me over the top into the gonna-go-for-it column.

First there was this conversation Friday afternoon with my favorite pastel person, Katie Lynn Kilroy. I was sitting there in English lit, minding my own business, doodling in the margin of my notebook, waiting for Frog Face Gerksky to show up for class—some teacher I didn't know had stuck her head in the door and said he'd be late—when I heard the unmistakable sound of Katie Lynn's titters behind me. I figured it was me she was tittering about, per usual. I ignored her, per usual.

The next thing I knew, she was sitting in the empty seat next to me. "Hey, Jane," she said in that sickly sweet southern drawl of hers. "Me and my friends were just talkin' about your outfit, which is so ... original."

I had on your basic East Village retro punk uni: black spandex leggings, a ripped T-shirt held together with tons of safety pins, an ancient black leather jacket with Day-Glo paint spattered here and there. I had added a pink streak to my hair, and I had six safety pins in my left ear instead of earrings, and a cute little plastic skull hanging from my right ear.

"Gee, yours too," I told her. "How did you ever think of matching your hair bow to your nail polish?"

Katie Lynn smiled sweetly. "Aren't you *amusin'!*" she exclaimed. She looked over at her friends, who were smirking at her; then she looked back at me. "Well, Jane, we were just wonderin', since you lived in New York and all, is it true that all the girls there sleep around with anything that walks, just to, you know, broaden their horizons?"

"Absolutely," I agreed. "My friends and I hit five, six bars a night and, like, jump up on the nearest pool table and offer to take on all comers."

"Well, bless your heart," Katie Lynn cooed. "And y'all don't worry about diseases?"

"Oh, no," I assured her airily. "Everyone in New York already has all those diseases, anyway."

"Well, don't you worry that people will think you have no morals?" she asked me, deep concern etched across her kittenish brow.

"Don't you worry that people will think you have no IQ?" I shot back.

Katie Lynn leaned closer. "I just think you should know that some people are sayin' you're, well, kind of a slut."

"*Some* people ought to get a life before they start talking about other people's," I snapped at her, my fists clenched in my lap.

Katie Lynn sighed. She traded another quick look with her buddies. "Jane, honey, if it walks like a duck and it quacks like a duck ..." She let the rest of the statement hang in the air, and gave me a little shrug. "I just thought you should know what people are sayin'."

She got up to go back to her friends, and from behind me I heard "quack-quack-quack" from a gaggle of pastel people.

I stared straight ahead. I wouldn't let them get

to me. I didn't care what they thought. I hated them with a pure white hatred.

And then I remembered something that Savy had told me just the day before. Katie Lynn Kilroy had gone out with Wyatt Shane once and only once, and he had dropped her flat. Everyone knew she wanted him. Well, *he* wanted *me*.

The second thing that happened was the phone call I got on Friday night at dinnertime from my former best friend from when I still had a life, Anita Lebowitz. My family was eating dinner. We were just digging in to my mother's mystery meat loaf when the phone rang. I ran to get it as my father yelled to me to tell whoever it was to call back because this was "family time." Well, it was Anita. Given a choice between talking to Anita and bonding with "Jilly" over Mom's mystery meat loaf, I ignored my dad's instructions and carried the cordless phone into the cubicle that passed as my room.

"Jane, I absolutely had to call you," Anita said dramatically.

I plopped down on my stomach on my bed and closed my eyes. Just for a moment I could pretend to be in my room in New York, on the phone with Anita, who lived just four blocks away, and in a few minutes Chad would come over and we'd go downtown to hear some music with all our friends and . . .

"... And I mean, I know it sucks, but I had to call and tell you!" Anita finished with a flourish.

Clearly I had zoned out there for just a moment. "Run that by me again," I suggested, rolling over onto my back.

"I *said* Chad is going out with Melanie Sherwin!" Anita repeated.

Melanie Sherwin. The biggest tease at Performing Arts. A great singer with long blond hair and body of death. Chad always told me she was too obvious. Obviously he had lied.

"Melanie Sherwin?" I repeated, aghast.

"You know that what Melanie wants, Melanie gets, and she wants *your* boyfriend!" Anita screeched. "You've got to figure out a way to get back here!"

"Sure, let me just hop in my Learjet," I said sarcastically. "How long has this been going on?"

"I saw them together at a party last weekend, but Chad told me they were just friends, that he still really loved you," Anita reported. "Then today I saw them sucking face in one of the practice studios at school. Chad saw me through the glass, and he looked really embarrassed. So then after school he, like, corners me in front of Woolworth's, and he goes 'Anita, what am I going to do? I think I'm in love with Melanie.'"

The slime lizard.

Okay, you may be saying to yourself, If Jane was so in love with this Chad guy why was she interested in Wyatt? What's good for the goose is good for the gander and all that. Well, Chad and I had a plan, see. We had discussed the whole thing. During the two years that we would be apart while I finished high school in Nashville, we could see other people. We just couldn't fall in *love* with other people. So here I'd been gone a few short weeks and Chad Berman, that fickle lowlife, was confiding in Anita that he was falling in love with Melanie Sherwin.

No wonder he hadn't answered my last three letters.

"Maybe it's just infatuation or something," I suggested hopefully to Anita.

"Jane, he's letting her sing with The Chill," Anita said.

My heart lurched like a stuck elevator. No one sang with The Chill but Chad. Not ever.

He really *did* love her.

We talked for another few minutes while I tried to come up with some desperate scheme to get Chad away from Melanie, but deep inside I knew it was beyond hopeless. Then my father came to my bedroom and used his "I mean business" voice to get me off the phone. Sure, he didn't care if my life was totally ruined. He cared more about the dubious nutritional value of mystery meat loaf.

Well, between these two catastrophic events, the writing was on the wall. I longed to do something to get back at Katie Lynn Kilroy, and my boyfriend, Chad, was a thousand miles away, in love with someone else.

I had absolutely nothing to lose by meeting Wyatt at that party, and maybe I even had something to gain. I was *not* somebody to trifle with. I was *not* somebody ordinary, average, normal, nice, sweet, or boring. I vowed I never would be.

And whatever else was true of Wyatt Shane, he wasn't, either.

"Your first party in Nashville," my mother said happily, as she watched me slipping silver earrings into my pierced ears. "Look how quickly you ended up making friends here after all!"

It was Sunday night and my mom was sitting on my bed watching me get ready for the party. I had told my parents that I'd been invited to this girl's party, that I knew her from school. I even made up a name for her—Lorraine Beecham. Where I got that name I haven't a clue. Wyatt hadn't written down any name on the piece of paper he'd given me with the address. I also told my parents I was going to the party with some girlfriends and I was giving my friend Savy a ride. My mom was so tickled over the whole thing that she'd agreed to let me take her vintage 240-Z, a car she cherished second only to her family. She was planning to use my car to drive Jill and her friend to the movies.

"It's just a stupid party," I said irritably, mostly because I felt so guilty about lying to her.

"Well, I'm sure you'll have fun," my mom said.

I slipped a black T-shirt over my head and then dropped a half dozen long pendants around my neck—peace symbols, crystals, yin and yang, that kind of stuff. I stepped into a black stretch miniskirt and then sat on the bed to lace up my black platform ankle boots.

"Very New York," Mom commented.

"I guess," I mumbled. I wished she wouldn't sit there, just watching me get dressed. I wished she wouldn't *care* so much about everything.

"Kids don't wear as much black here, do they?" she said conversationally.

"I do," I replied tersely.

Mom sighed. "Sometimes I just don't know how to talk to you anymore, Jane."

She looked so sad. I felt bad at the way I was treating her and irritated with her at the same time. Why couldn't she just let me *be?*

"I'm sorry, Mom," I said, sitting next to her on the bed. "I'm just nervous ... about the party."

"Oh, I understand," my mother assured me, eager to accept my apology. Sure, it was the first civil thing I'd said to her in days.

I smiled at her, the dutiful daughter.

She didn't understand anything at all.

I was nervous, that much was true, but it wasn't about the party, about which I couldn't have cared less. I was nervous because I had neglected to inform Wyatt of one teeny little detail about myself. He thought I was very cool, very experienced and worldly. I mean, girls had to be faster in New York, right? Everyone thought that. Well, I guess I let them think that. Actually, I guess I *led* them to think that. The truth of the matter was . . . I was a virgin.

Gawd, is that dull or what?

See, Chad was my first really serious boyfriend. We'd started going together the middle of our sophomore year. I definitely hadn't been ready then. Maybe if we'd stayed together, we would have eventually gone all the way. I guess I'll never know now. But the thing is, I really, really wanted to be in love when I finally *made* love. And I saw all these kids having sex, thinking they were so madly in love, and then a few weeks later they were, like, "Oh, I can't stand him anymore." And it turned out it hadn't been real love at all. I'm not even sure I know what real love is, if you want to know the truth. And I wasn't about to have sex until I figured it out.

Um, I guess this is a little detail I hadn't exactly mentioned to Wyatt.

Silly me.

I got into Mom's car and headed for Belle Meade, the very ritziest section of Nashville. I had checked a map, and easily found Chickering Lane, where the party was taking place. I drove slowly down the curvy street, staring at the incredibly huge houses set far back on stately lawns. They were the biggest houses I'd ever seen in my life. Unbelievable. Most of the houses were traditional-looking, but one looked like a white spaceship about to take off. A huge sculpture and fountain decorated the immense front lawn. Since I come from a city where even the richest people live on top of each other in high-rises and where "land" consists of a garden apartment where a wilting flower or two might be coaxed to bloom, all of these mansions and green hills were kind of, well, intimidating.

Telling myself they didn't have the Metropolitan Museum of Art, the Metropolitan Opera, or the New York Mets, I pulled into a driveway that led up to a pink stucco mansion.

Gulp.

The driveway was already full of cars, and heavy metal music blasted from inside the house.

Some kids were on the huge front porch, screaming, laughing, dancing. Everyone knew everyone, and I didn't know anyone. Two cute guys walked by my car and checked it out, clearly impressed. They looked at me behind the steering wheel and gave me that "looking good" kind of smile. I knew it was dumb, but that smile helped my confidence. I took a deep breath and got out of the car.

There must have been a hundred kids inside that house. And what a house. A sunken living room bigger than our entire apartment ran to the left off the circular front hall. A couple with beers in their hands were standing on a white couch, kissing. A group of kids stood around a short girl who was chugging shots of vodka while they egged her on chanting, "Chug! Chug! Chug!"

I made my way through the crowd, heading for the music. I walked down a hall, past an open bedroom door. A couple were on the bed getting hot and heavy, oblivious to the open door. I heard someone barfing in what I figured was the bathroom. I passed an aquarium where a stoned guy had a joint in one hand and was fishing fishies out of the tank with the other. Then he popped a fish into his mouth. And swallowed.

None of this was my idea of a really swell time.

At the end of the hall were some stairs, and

as I walked down them the music got louder and louder, until I entered the main party room.

Did you ever see that painting of hell, by some artist named Dali? Well, Dali must have gone to a similar party, and then put the sucker on some canvas. I've been to wild parties in my life, but this one was out of control. It was very clear that no parents were anywhere in the vicinity. Every kind of drug and all forms of alcohol were being consumed. A guy bumped into me, carrying over his shoulder a girl who had passed out.

"Where you goin' with Patti, man?" someone called to him.

"The bedroom, dude!" the guy yelled back.

"Go for it!" a couple of guys hooted back at him.

I was pretty sure poor Patti didn't have a lot to say about where she was headed. I started to feel sick to my stomach.

I was thinking about leaving, I really was. But then I saw Wyatt at the other side of the room, playing lead guitar with his band. He saw me and caught my eye. And he gave me a huge dazzling grin.

I grinned back. I couldn't help it.

I listened to his band, Thunder Rolls, as they rocked out. Wyatt had been telling me the truth—they really *were* good. As soon as they finished the tune, Wyatt leaned into the mike and said, "We'll be back in a few." Then he headed right for me. Somebody slipped a cassette into the sound system and an old Doors tape blasted out.

"Well, well, well, you came," he yelled at me over the music, clearly pleased. He leaned over and kissed my cheek, which I thought was sweet. He had a beer in one hand, and I caught a quick whiff of alcohol on his breath.

"Whose house is this?" I yelled. A drunk guy knocked an expensive-looking lamp off a table, and it crashed to the floor. Some people applauded.

"Just some rich girl's," Wyatt yelled. He grabbed my hand, and it felt like an electric current ran through my fingers. He looked at me and I looked back at him. I knew he wanted to kiss me. And I knew I wanted to kiss him. "Come on," he urged me, leading me to who-knew-where.

Everything felt dangerous.

I went.

CHAPTER
9

💗

Wyatt led me out through a sliding glass door, past a huge swimming pool where twenty or so kids were cavorting in and around the water. Two boys holding a girl by her hands and feet swung her fully clothed into the pool. Some of the kids in the water looked like they were naked, and various clothing was strewn around the sides of the pool.

"This is cheap swill, man," one guy said as he emptied the bottle of champagne into the shallow end of the pool.

The backyard seemed to go on forever. Wyatt led me past tennis courts, past a fountain and a pond, until finally the noise of the party was distant and I could hear an owl hooting from one of the trees. I leaned back against the tree and looked at his silhouette outlined by the full moon above us.

"Better?" he asked me.

"Better," I agreed, with a warm feeling in my heart. Somehow he'd known I didn't want to be at that insane party.

"So . . ." Wyatt said, studying me with a be-mused look on his face. He lifted his beer and took a long swallow, then he held it out to me.

I shook my head no.

"Don't tell me a fast girl like you from New York doesn't drink," he teased.

I shrugged as if such things were too banal for me to bother about. The fact of the matter is I don't drink. Alcohol makes me feel sick, and most of the time it seems to make people act really, really dumb, although they seem to think they are being very cool.

"Your band sounded pretty good," I told Wyatt.

"Oh, you approve, huh?" he asked me, a smile playing around his lips.

"Well, your drummer needs work," I added honestly. "And your bass player isn't very original."

Irritation flicked over his face. "You listened for maybe thirty seconds and you know, huh?"

I shrugged again.

Wyatt took another long pull at his beer, then

turned the bottle upside down. The last few drops trickled onto the grass. He put the bottle down at the foot of the tree, then leaned one arm over me, the same way he had at school. His face was very close to mine. Now I could really smell the alcohol on his breath. He'd clearly had a few brews before the one he'd just finished. I couldn't decide if it was sexy or disgusting.

"So, do the girls in New York know how to kiss?" Wyatt asked me softly.

"I guess that would be a matter of opinion," I replied, my heart racing in my chest.

Slowly he leaned down and gave me a soft, sexy kiss. He didn't grab me or force his tongue into my mouth or do any of those disgusting things boys sometimes do right off because they think it's macho or something equally repulsive.

"You taste good," Wyatt murmured.

"You taste like beer," I murmured back.

Wyatt laughed. "You just won't cut me a break, will you, tough girl?" He leaned over and kissed me again. This time his arms went around my waist, gently pulling me to him.

I wrapped my arms around his neck and kissed him back until we were both breathless. It felt fabulous. I didn't want to think about what I was doing, about the fact that I didn't even know Wyatt or the fact that everyone said he was major bad news. I loved to kiss him, and nobody was going to stop me.

"I think we need more privacy than this, don't you?" Wyatt asked me in a gruff, passion-tinged voice.

"There's no one here but us and that owl who keeps hooting," I told him, brazenly kissing his neck.

"Yeah, well, I'm not much of a nature boy," he told me. "I prefer a nice firm bed."

Bed? Did he say *bed*?

Wyatt took my hand and started to lead me back toward the house.

"I really like it out here," I told him, hanging back by the tree.

"You'll like it better in a bed, I promise," he replied with a sexy grin.

"I thought you had to play another set," I said, stalling for time.

He put his arms back around my waist and nuzzled my neck. "You think anyone back there is still straight enough to know if it's the band or the tapes?"

"Well, you guys don't sound like the Doors," I pointed out nervously. "They're playing Doors tapes. So, do you think Jim Morrison was a poet? The voice of a generation? Or do you think he was just really self-destructive? I mean, how would you compare him to, say, Jimi Hendrix?"

"Jane—" Wyatt began.

"I really, really wish I'd been alive to go to Woodstock," I continued babbling.

Wyatt stepped closer.

"It's kind of amazing that David Crosby is even still alive, don't you think?" I added lamely. "I mean, he really abused his body and—"

Wyatt kissed me to shut me up. It was a great kiss, a sizzling kiss, a kiss that made my knees and my willpower weak at the same time. When he stopped kissing me—which may have been five minutes or an hour later, since it felt so good that I lost track of the time—he just took my hand again and led me back toward the house.

Right near the pool a boy and a girl were all over each other. It looked as though she had stripped down to her panties, but it was too dark to know for sure. But seeing that shook me out of my temporary lust-induced stupor.

"Hey, let's go for a ride!" I suggested, since it was the first thing that popped into my mind as an alternative to the bedroom.

"I have something else in mind," Wyatt told me, running his hand down my back. "You do, too."

"Ever drive a vintage 240-Z?" I asked Wyatt quickly.

Wyatt's face lit up. "You have a vintage 240-Z?"

I nodded yes, neglecting to mention that it happened to belong to my mother, who got a great deal on it because of my father's job at Nissan.

"Come on." I led him around the house to my mother's car, which gleamed cherry red under the spotlight over the driveway.

"Woah," Wyatt breathed, running his hand over the perfect finish on the hood. "This baby is fine."

"Nice wheels, Wyatt," another guy said, coming out of the house with his arm around a petite dark-haired girl. He had two beers in his hands, and he handed one to the girl. She made a face and pushed it away, so the guy handed it to Wyatt. "That your car, man?"

"No, it's hers," Wyatt said, putting his arm around my neck.

"Cool," the guy said with approval, then he sauntered off with the girl.

Wyatt popped open the beer and took a swig, then reached for my hand and tugged in the direction of the house. Obviously the car had not totally dissuaded him from the bedroom concept.

"Want to drive it?" I offered quickly. I reached into the back pocket of my jeans and dangled the car keys off my finger.

Wyatt grinned and grabbed the keys.

We got into the car—Wyatt behind the steering wheel—and he turned on the engine. There were so many cars around it that the only way he could get out of the driveway was to go up on the grass, which he did. He turned on the radio as loud as it would go as we hit Chickering Lane, and he pressed down on the gas pedal.

"Far-friggin' out!" Wyatt cried as the car sped up easily to seventy miles an hour. He took another long drink from his beer.

"Maybe you shouldn't drink and drive," I suggested, reaching for the can.

"It's only a brew!" he replied with a derisive laugh.

"Yeah, but—"

"Hey, lighten up!" Wyatt suggested, putting his arm around me and cradling his beer between his legs. "This car is unreal."

Wyatt headed down dark, empty streets, speeding the car up to eighty, then ninety miles an hour.

"Listen, I really think you should slow down," I said nervously.

Wyatt gave me an amused look. "You scared?"

"I just think this is stupid," I replied.

He laughed and pressed down on the gas pedal. The speedometer needle headed up into the ninety-five-mile-an-hour range.

"I mean it, Wyatt, slow down," I said sharply. He didn't. How many beers had he had before I even showed up at the party? Was he drunk? Was it safe for him to be driving at all? All of a sudden I couldn't believe I'd gotten myself into this mess, all because I didn't want to tell him that I wouldn't go into the bedroom with him.

"Woah, baby!" Wyatt hooted. "I am in love with this sucker!" He took a turn too fast, and the wheels screeched around the bend.

"Slow down or I will kill you, I mean it!" I screamed over the radio.

He gave me a quick look. "Your wish is my command," he said lazily, and brought the car down to a normal speed. I heaved a huge sigh of relief. Then he made a turn down a dark, narrow road, slowed the car down in a grove of trees, and stopped.

It was so quiet I could hear the beating of my own heart. "I'm driving back," I told him.

"Cool," he agreed easily, reaching for his beer. He took a long drink. "Didn't you get off on that adrenaline rush?"

"No," I said bluntly.

"Hey, you're really pissed," he realized.

"No kidding," I snapped.

"I'm sorry," Wyatt said, pulling me to him. "Really." He kissed me softly until I gave in and started kissing him back. "Better?" he murmured.

I nodded into his chest.

He kissed me some more. It was great, and we were both getting really turned on. Slowly I felt his hand heading for my breasts. I shifted positions so he reached for my arm instead. After a few more intense kisses he reached for my breast again. This time I felt his hand on my T-shirt, over my bra. My body was into it, but my mind went on red alert.

"Hey, let's just chill out for a while," I suggested breathlessly, moving away from him.

"That's like throwing water on a grease fire," Wyatt murmured. "It just sends the flames higher." He reached for me again.

I kissed him. It felt so great. How could it feel so great to be kissing this guy I didn't even know? But it did, and I didn't want to think about it. So I didn't.

Until I felt Wyatt's hand edging under my skirt.

I grabbed his wrist.

"Uh, I don't think that's a really good idea," I whispered.

"Oh, yeah, it is," he replied, reaching under my skirt again.

"No, it isn't," I insisted, pulling his hand out. I leaned forward for more kisses.

"Come on, babe, you don't have to play that coy game with me," Wyatt said roughly. "We both know what we came here for."

"We were just going to take a ride in my car—"

"No, we were going to go to the bedroom and

get down," Wyatt corrected me. "We just ended up in the car first." I felt his hand inching up my thigh.

"Stop it. I mean it," I told him irritably, pulling his hand away.

He reached for the bottom of my T-shirt and jerked it up over my bra.

"Cut it out!" I yelled, struggling away from him, smoothing down my T-shirt.

"You are nothing but a damn tease!" Wyatt yelled. "If there's one thing I can't stand it's a damn tease!" He pulled me to him roughly, and I struggled away from him, hitting at his hand.

Suddenly I realized how drunk he was. *Really* drunk. Why hadn't I let myself truly believe that before? This whole thing was just crazy! I had to have been insane to let him drive my mom's car drunk!

"Come here," Wyatt demanded, reaching for me again. He grabbed my arm hard but I shook it off.

"Forget it!" I yelled. "Just forget it!" I felt like crying. How had something that had started out so great turned into something so ugly?

"You stupid tease," Wyatt snarled at me. "You want it. You just don't want to admit you want it!"

"Get out of the car," I ordered him, reaching for the door handle on my side. "We're leaving and I'm driving." I got out and slammed the car door and walked around the car.

But Wyatt didn't get out of the car.

Instead he started the motor.

"Wyatt!" I yelled, reaching for his door handle.

But before my hand made contact with the handle, Wyatt put the car into gear, stepped on the gas pedal, and sped off into the night.

Drunk.

In my mother's car.

Leaving me alone. In the dark. By the side of the road. In the middle of nowhere.

I was dead meat.

CHAPTER
10

♡

For a moment I just stood there. I couldn't believe what had just happened. I had absolutely no idea where I was. There wasn't a soul in sight. I shivered in the night air.

Caw! Caw!

I jumped in fright as a large bird took wing through the trees.

Okay, Jane, you're in Nashville. Somewhere. This is not like being left in Central Park at midnight, I told myself.

I walked out into the road and peered to the right, then to the left. Which way was closer to civilization? I tried to remember how far we'd driven since our turnoff from the main road. Had it been a mile? Two miles? More? I looked in the opposite direction. Was that way closer to a main road and a pay phone?

I had no idea. I wanted to cry, but knew it wouldn't get me anywhere. I took a deep breath and started back in the direction in which Wyatt had taken off with my car.

I was going to kill him.

That is, if my parents didn't kill me first.

After walking for maybe ten minutes I came to a farmhouse. The front porch light was on. Should I go up there and knock, plead my case, and ask to use their phone?

In New York people got murdered for taking that kind of a detour.

I trudged on.

As I walked, I ran the evening over and over in my mind. How could I have been so incredibly dumb? How could I have trusted Wyatt after everyone told me not to? How could I have let him drive when he'd been drinking? And how the hell had I managed to let him drive off with my mother's car?

Finally, after about a half hour on that dark, lonely road where not one car passed me, I came to a main road. Franklin Road, the sign said. I looked down the road, and in the distance I could just make out the neon lights of a Texaco station.

Thank you, God.

I trudged along the side of the road until I got to the gas station, where surely I could make a phone call.

It was closed.

Now I couldn't stop myself from crying. God, I was so screwed. I looked at my watch under a streetlight. It was one-thirty in the morning. My parents had to be really worried, since I never stayed out past midnight without calling them. And on a school night I never stayed out past midnight, period.

I brushed the tears off my cheek with the back of my hand and looked around dismally.

"Why isn't there a stupid pay phone here?" I yelled out loud. I swore under my breath. I hated this town. At least if I was in New York something would be open. Something was *always* open in New York.

In the distance I heard the sound of a car, then saw the headlights. It was a black sports car, sleek, new. Whoever was driving saw me, slowed down, and turned into the gas station.

I gulped hard. My eyes darted around. What if it was some crazed pervert? New York is full of crazed perverts, but I was bright enough not to confront one on the street, alone, at one-thirty in the morning.

The car stopped.

Should I make a run for it? Where would I run *to*?

I needed a weapon. I reached into my back pocket for my keys, but of course they weren't there because Wyatt had them. There was nothing there but my wallet and a hair pick.

I grabbed the hair pick and held it tight, ready to spring into action.

The car door opened.

I took off—it was reflex. I started running down the road.

"Hey! Hey there, do you need some help?" a male voice called to me.

I was far enough away to risk turning around. If he got into his car to follow me I planned to throw myself into the woods on the side of the road and run as if my life depended on it, which might actually be the case.

"I said do you need some help?" he called to me again. He reached into his car for something. A gun? But no, it was a phone. "You need to call someone?" he yelled.

From where I was I couldn't make out his face or read his intentions. Was he saving my butt or would he turn into a maniac at any moment? Whoever he was, he was driving an expensive car and he had a car phone.

"We need to make a call," I said guardedly. "My boyfriend is just back there," I added, cocking my head toward the gas station. I hoped he believed that I wasn't alone.

"Well, y'all can use this phone," the man said.

I was afraid to move.

"Look, miss, I only stopped because I saw you standing there looking upset. I've got a daughter your age."

Was it the truth or a trap? I took a few steps toward him.

"Want me to dial for you so you know it's okay?" he called to me.

I called out our phone number to him.

"I'm dialing," he said. "Who should I say is calling?"

"Tell them Jane," I shouted.

"Hello, sir, I'm calling for Jane," I heard him say into the phone.

"Ask the person's name," I yelled to the man, just in case he was scamming me.

"Jane wants me to ask who is speaking," the man said into the phone. He listened for a moment. "Jim McVay," the man called to me.

I let go of the breath I hadn't even realized I was holding and ran to the car.

"Thanks," I told the man gratefully when he handed me his phone. He smiled at me. Now I could see his kind face.

"Daddy?" I said into the phone.

"Jane? What the hell is going on?" my dad yelled. "Who was that man? Where are you?"

I closed my eyes. They were going to kill me. "I'm on Franklin Road ... somewhere," I said lamely.

"I thought you were at a party," my father said.

"I was," I told him, "but I ... I ..." How could I possibly explain? This was by far the worst thing that had ever happened to me. "I went for a drive with a friend, and ... he took off with Mom's car," I finally managed to say.

"He *what?*" my father exploded.

"I got out and told him I had to drive, and he just ... took off," I said. "So I walked to a gas station but it was closed and there wasn't a pay phone, and then this man stopped and said I could use his car phone."

"You're standing in the middle of nowhere in the middle of the night using some strange man's car phone?"

"Please don't yell, Daddy—"

"I'm coming to get you right now," my father said. "Where are you, exactly?"

"Excuse me," I asked the man. "Where am I, exactly?"

"Texaco station, Franklin Road near Holly Tree Gap Road," the man said. "It's about a half mile before the Legends Golf Course in Franklin."

I relayed this information to my father.

"Don't move, don't breathe, just wait there for me," my father instructed me. "I'll be right there." Then he hung up.

I handed the phone back to the man. "Thanks," I told him. "My father is coming to get me." Tears were coursing down my cheeks. I just couldn't stop myself from crying. Everything was so messed up.

"Would you feel safer if I waited here with you until your dad got here?" the man asked me kindly.

I nodded yes.

We stood there together in silence; the only sound was me choking on my own snotty tears. The man reached into his car and handed me a box of Kleenex. I took out a few and blew my nose loudly.

"You know, my daughter, Karen, once stayed out all night," he said. "She didn't call. Her momma was so worried I thought the woman would have a heart attack. But it turned out Karen had just fallen asleep at her friend's house. I was so mad at her for being that inconsiderate to her momma I'd have liked to tan her hide. But, well, I didn't. It passed. It wasn't the end of the world."

"This is," I sniffed, blowing my nose again.

"Parents have a way of forgivin' their children," the man said gently. "You'll see."

In no time at all my father's car pulled up to the gas station. Both my parents were inside.

"Get in this car," my father said to me in the coldest voice I had ever heard him use.

"Thanks for your help," I told the man.

He smiled at me and got into his car, and I got into the back seat of my dad's car. He started driving. "Now, I want you to tell your mother and me exactly what happened tonight from the beginning, so that it actually makes some sense," my father said in a tight voice.

I told them the whole story. I suppose I cleaned it up a little—like I left out the part about the bedroom, and I didn't mention that Wyatt had been drinking. I just couldn't bring myself to tell them that.

"What is this kid, crazy?" my father yelled.

"He just took off with my car and left you by the side of the road?" my mother questioned, her voice edged with hysteria. "Was he drinking?"

"I don't know," I hedged.

"Jane McVay, was this kid drinking?" my father demanded. "I want an honest answer, dammit!"

"Yes," I said miserably.

"Oh, Jane," my mother sighed.

That was the worst, hearing the terrible disappointment in her voice.

My father pulled into our spot in the parking lot, and we walked into our apartment. "Get this kid on the phone," my father said in an exhausted voice.

I glanced at my watch. "But it's two o'clock in the morning," I protested.

"Just do it," my father said. "Now."

I looked up Wyatt's number in the phone book, praying that he wasn't listed, but there it was—Randall Shane, on Abbott Martin. And underneath that was Wyatt Shane at the same address. Evidently he had his own phone.

I pushed the buttons on the phone for Wyatt's number and listened to the rings.

Click.

"Hey, you know who it is and you know what to do," his sexy recorded voice said.

"It's Jane," I said into the phone. I looked over at my father.

"Tell him to bring the car to school tomorrow, and then I want him over here so I can speak with him."

"Bring my car to school tomorrow," I said, "and, uh, my father would like to speak with you."

"And I want to speak with his parents. Tell him that," my father said.

"And your parents," I added into the phone. Then I hung up.

Clearly my life was over.

I was afraid my father would make me call

Wyatt's parents' number, but fortunately he didn't realize it was a different number.

My parents were sitting on the couch, speaking with each other in low tones.

"I let you take my car and you took terrible advantage of the situation," my mother finally said. "We are very, very angry and disappointed."

"I know," I whispered miserably.

"And this kid, drinking and driving," my father said. "You let him do it, which makes you as bad as him in my book."

I nodded.

"Well, we're going to be speaking to this kid—what's his name?" my father asked.

"Wyatt Shane," I said, wishing I'd never heard the name in my life.

"And his parents. Tomorrow," my mother said firmly.

"Meanwhile this joker better have your mother's car at school tomorrow or I will go to the police," my father said. "As for you, except for school you are grounded for a month."

"Can I still play in the pit band for the school play?" I asked them. "I mean, it's a school activity, and the other kids in the band will be screwed if I drop out now."

They conferred for a moment.

"Okay," my mother agreed. "But other than school and band practice, you are home, period."

I nodded. There was no point in arguing. I was totally screwed. "Can I go to bed now?"

"Go," my father said. He sounded totally disgusted with me.

Well, he couldn't possibly be any more disgusted with me than I was with myself.

It was only my being so pissed at Wyatt that kept me from being a nervous wreck the next day. Nobody, but nobody, had ever done anything to me as bad as what he'd done to me. I was going to kill him, which was justice, since he deserved to die.

Jill managed to worm the whole story out of my mother, and she looked at me wide-eyed when I came to breakfast. The tension in our breakfast nook was so thick you could cut it with a knife. Jill kept her mouth shut, which was a good thing, or she would have been my first homicide.

My mother drove Jill and me to school so she'd have my car. She drove silently, then stopped in front of school and turned to me. "I expect that boy, with my car, to come to our house the instant school is out today," she said. "And I expect to see his parents this evening."

"Maybe we could leave his parents out of this," I tried meekly.

"No chance," my mother said tersely. "What

he did was criminal. Either we talk with his parents or we go straight to the police. We may end up going to the police in any event; your father and I haven't decided yet."

I sighed and got out of the car. My mother zoomed off. She could be very tough when she really wanted to be.

I went to the science wing because I knew Wyatt's first class was advanced biology, but he wasn't there yet. So I went to World Lit and sat through a boring discussion about imagery in poetry. Then I ran back to the science wing.

I watched everyone filing out of the room. No Wyatt. Maybe I had just missed him.

"Hey, was Wyatt in class?" I asked his friend Mike.

"Nope," Mike told me, shaking his hair out of his eyes. "His mom called me this morning. Bad news, man. Wyatt was out with some babe last night and got into a car accident."

"Oh, God—" slipped out of my mouth.

Mike grinned. "I didn't know you cared so much."

I didn't. I cared about my mother's car. "Is he okay?" I asked.

"Yeah," Mike replied, "except he broke his arm in two places, which is a bummer, 'cuz he can't play guitar, ya know?"

"The car . . . ?"

Mike shrugged. "It must have been the babe's

car, because Wyatt totaled his wheels last year, and his parents refuse to cough up for a new one. That's all I know, except I'm supposed to get his homework."

I walked down the hall in a daze. Oh, my God. He had wrecked my mother's car. I had to call his house and find out what had happened. I ran to the pay phones near the gym, called information for Wyatt's number, and pushed the digits into the phone.

His answering machine came on.

I got his parents' number and tried that, but all I got was another answering machine.

No way out, no way out.

I walked right out of school. I couldn't face class when my life was passing before my eyes. I walked around for a couple of hours, then decided to go back. It was lunchtime now; maybe someone would know something. And I could try Wyatt's number again.

I found Kimmy and Savy in the cafeteria, eating lunch.

"Hi, I thought you weren't in school," Savy said with surprise. She was slicing a large piece of Gramma Beth's strudel in half.

"Take that knife and slit my wrists," I said, sitting down next to Savy.

"What happened?" Kimmy asked. "You look awful."

I told the two of them what had happened with Wyatt the night before. Then I told them what Mike had told me this morning. The more I got into the story, the paler both of their faces got.

"He was with *you?*" Kimmy whispered, wide-eyed. "We thought it had to be his girlfriend, Brenda."

"He has a *girlfriend?*" I asked incredulously. "That cretin actually has a *girlfriend?*" Things kept getting worse and worse.

Kimmy nodded. "Her name is Brenda Pirkell. She went here last year, but then she transferred to some Christian school. She's really wild. And Wyatt cheats on her all the time."

"Listen, Jane, things are even worse than you know," Savy said, putting her hand on my arm.

"They can't get any worse," I told her.

"Well, maybe what we heard isn't true—" she began.

"It's only a rumor," Kimmy added.

"But, well, Gil Prentis's mom is a doctor in the emergency room at Vanderbilt," Savy said, "and she told Gil that Wyatt was in a drunk-driving accident last night and he hit another car. There were two girls in the other car, and they were admitted in serious condition."

I put my head down on the table. No. This absolutely could not be happening. I lifted my head and looked at Savy. "How serious?" I whispered.

"I don't know. He just said 'serious,'" Savy reported, her eyes filled with compassion.

"Hey, I need to talk to you," Sandra Farrell said, slipping into the seat next to Kimmy. "I need to change band practice this week. I have to do this seminar at—" Then she saw the looks on our faces. "Did someone die?" she asked.

"Oh, God!" I cried pitifully and put my head down again. What if someone actually *did* die? What if one of those girl from the other car already *had?* It would be my fault, just as much as if I'd been driving the car.

"Jane is just a little upset," Savy explained.

"What the hell am I going to do?" I moaned, looking from face to face for some kind of answer.

"A little?" Sandra asked, raising her eyebrows.

"Can I tell her?" Savy asked me.

I nodded mutely.

Savy related the horror story to Sandra.

"Wow," Sandra said. She looked thoughtful for a moment. "You called Wyatt's house?" she asked me.

I nodded again. "No answer."

"Well, either he's home and not answering or he's still at the hospital," Sandra said. "Either way you've got to find him, right?"

"Right," I agreed. "If I had my car here I'd drive over to his house and see if he's there, but I don't."

Sandra gave me an appraising look. "I've got my Jeep," she said evenly.

I stared at her. "What about school?"

"What about it?" she asked me. "You want a ride to Wyatt's house or don't you?"

"I do!" I said quickly.

"Well, then, let's go," she said, getting up.

"I'm coming, too." Savy stood up. "That is, if it's okay."

"I'll take all the moral support I can get," I told her gratefully.

"I guess you wouldn't want me along," Kimmy said in a low voice, staring at the table.

"You don't have to cut school for me," I told her, "but if you want to come, I want you along."

"Really?" she asked hopefully.

"Kimmy, no one has time to stroke your ego right now," Sandra said, folding her arms. "Are you in or not?"

"I'm in," Kimmy decided in a tremulous voice.

The four of us strode out of school and headed for Sandra's Jeep.

Savy squeezed my hand and I squeezed back.

Whatever horror I was about to face, at least I wasn't facing it alone.

CHAPTER
11

⟨♡⟩

*T*hat's Wyatt's house," Kimmy said, when we turned the corner onto Abbott Martin.

She pointed to a white ranch house on the corner with red flowers in the flower beds and a swing on the front porch. It looked so normal. You'd never know the scum of the earth lived there.

"How come you know where Wyatt lives?" I asked Kimmy as Sandra pulled her Jeep into his driveway.

"Oh, uh, well . . ." Kimmy stammered, blushing furiously.

"Don't tell me you went out with him, too," Sandra said, turning off the engine.

"Oh, no!" Kimmy insisted. "Someone showed me once, that's all."

I shrugged. Kimmy sometimes said the strangest things. Well, I didn't have time to dwell on it. I had to go up to the front door and see if Wyatt was there.

I rang the bell, Sandra, Savy, and Kimmy standing right behind me. No one answered.

Sandra peered through the glass part of the garage door. "There's a car in here, for whatever that's worth."

"Try ringing again," Savy suggested.

I rang the bell again, long and hard, then I pounded on the door with my fist, and even kicked it with my shoe. Nothing.

"So maybe that means he was admitted to the hospital," Sandra said.

"Well, we know it's Vanderbilt," Savvy put in. "We could go over there."

My stomach was all tied up in knots. If Wyatt had been admitted to the hospital, maybe he'd been more seriously hurt than Mike had told me. And what about the two girls in the other car?

I pounded on the door again in frustration, and then to my surprise it slowly opened.

There stood Wyatt, shirtless, in a pair of baggy jeans. His arm was in a cast. He looked sleepy and out of it.

"You woke me up," he said groggily, running his left hand—the one without the cast—through his messy hair. "They gave me some stuff at the hospital to make me sleep."

"What happened last night?" I asked him, folding my arms in front of me. "You have a hell of a lot of explaining to do."

"Oh, yeah?" Wyatt sneered. "Like you didn't totally ruin my life last night?"

"I ruined *your* life?" I screeched. This guy was unbelievable! "You left me standing by the side of a dirt road in the middle of the night, stole my mother's car, and got into a drunk-driving accident, and you're telling me *I ruined your life?*"

"How do you know about that?" Wyatt asked sullenly.

"Gee, good news about you just flew around school this morning," I told him. "You were in an accident, right?"

"Yeah," Wyatt admitted.

"Was anyone hurt?" I asked him anxiously.

"Yeah, me!" he exclaimed.

"This guy is some piece of work," Sandra muttered under her breath.

"Oh, you think breaking my arm in two places so that I can't play the guitar is nothing?" Wyatt demanded, evidently having overheard Sandra.

"Jane meant was anyone else hurt," Savy explained in an even voice.

Wyatt couldn't quite look at me. "Two girls

from Hillsboro High were in the other car," he mumbled. "One of 'em has a bunch of cuts and stuff. The other one broke her collarbone and her leg."

"Oh, my God!" I cried, clapping my hand over my mouth. "You hit their car with my mother's car?"

"Hey, if you hadn't been such a little tease, none of this would have happened!" Wyatt yelled at me. "You think I wanted to hurt anybody?"

"Where is my mother's car?" I demanded.

"You told me it was your car," Wyatt said.

"Where is it?" I repeated.

"I had it towed to the Gulf station on West End," Wyatt said, running his hand through his hair again. "It's pretty wrecked."

"You are the lowest person I have ever met in my life," I seethed. "I loathe you."

"Yeah, well, ditto," he shot back at me.

"Look, my parents want to speak with you and your parents," I said.

"Well, the yokes are off on a cruise, so too bad for you," Wyatt replied snottily.

I grabbed a pen and a piece of paper from my purse and thrust it at him. "Write down the names of the girls you hit," I told him.

He wrote quickly and awkwardly with his left hand, then thrust it back at me.

"My parents might go to the police," I warned Wyatt. "It's what you deserve."

"Hey, they can get in line, okay?" Wyatt smirked. "The two bimbos in the other car are pressing charges. The cops gave me a Breathalyzer test, which I flunked. I am in deep dung, babe. I hope you're proud of yourself."

"Don't blame me for your—" I began.

"Here's a little piece of advice," Wyatt interrupted. "Next time you come on like you're all ready, willing, and able, don't come on to me."

"I never came on to you."

"Like hell you didn't," Wyatt snarled. "Just get out of my life."

He slammed the door in my face.

"I don't believe it," I said, standing there, facing a closed door. I kicked the door as hard as I could. Twice.

"Believe it," Sandra said flatly.

We walked back to Sandra's Jeep and sat there, silent.

"What now?" Savy asked.

No one had a ready answer.

Sandra started the Jeep and headed back toward school.

In my mind I went over how ugly Wyatt had just been. There was something seriously wrong with the guy. But I felt just awful enough and just guilty enough to let some of his words sink in. I really *did* blame myself.

I gulped hard so that I wouldn't start crying. "Savy, I should have listened to you about Wyatt. Then none of this would have happened."

"Hey, don't start blaming yourself for what he did," Savy exclaimed.

"I ... I thought maybe you were wrong about him," I continued, refusing to be let off the hook when I felt so guilty. "And my boyfriend back home is in love with someone else, and Wyatt kept flirting with me ..." A tear slid out of one eye and fell on my cheek.

"Oh, well, that's an excellent reason to let the drunk fool drive your mother's car," Sandra said sarcastically.

"Haven't you ever made a mistake?" I cried.

Sandra gave me a cool look.

"No, I don't suppose you ever have," I said, answering my own question.

"Don't be so hard on yourself," Savy insisted. "So many girls have fallen for his line of b.s."

"Well, I'm smarter than that," I replied. "No, I guess I'm not smarter than that. God, I'd like to kill him!"

"Look, I know you're feeling bad," Sandra said, pulling into the school parking lot, "but we need an action plan here. You can beat yourself up later."

"Sandra!" Savy chided her. "Jane is really upset!"

"No, Sandra's right," I insisted, brushing the tears off my face. "The first thing I need to do is call the two girls Wyatt hurt. And I'm going to have to tell my mother her car is wrecked. She's going to kill me. She already grounded me for a month."

"Does that mean you can't play in the pit band?" Savy asked quickly.

"I can play," I assured her. "It's school, the band, and my cell of a bedroom for the next thirty days. Now that my mom's car is wrecked, I'll probably be grounded for my entire life."

"Y'all, we have a bigger problem than that," Sandra pointed out. "We no longer have a guitar player. And I don't need to remind you that dress rehearsal is tomorrow night."

"There was silence in the car. As if on cue, Sandra, Savy, and I all turned to Kimmy.

"Oh, no," Kimmy exclaimed. "Forget it! Just forget it!"

"We can't forget it," Savy insisted. "There is no one else in the school who could learn those charts overnight. If you won't do it, we won't have a lead guitar for the pit band."

"Okay, you won't have a lead guitar," Kimmy said, nervously pushing her glasses up her nose.

"Without a lead guitar, there *is* no pit band," Sandra stated flatly.

"Y'all, this is totally not fair!" Kimmy cried. "I just cannot do this!"

" 'Can't,' my butt," Sandra snapped. "You mean 'won't,' so just say 'won't.' "

Kimmy cowered in the back seat. "I really, really do not think I'm good enough," she whispered.

"But you are!" Savy insisted. "You know I wouldn't lie to you!"

Kimmy twisted the material of her skirt anxiously between her fingers. "Last week my father came to my room while I was playing," she said in a low voice. "He banged on the door and yelled at me to stop the awful noise."

"Well, what does he know?" I scoffed.

She gave me a miserable look. "My father is first chair violinist for the symphony."

"Oh," I replied meekly.

"So, that doesn't mean the man knows rock 'n' roll!" Sandra pointed out.

"My mother told me she'd pay me to give up electric guitar," Kimmy continued. "She said she'd buy me any kind of car I wanted. Or I could have a trip to Europe. All I had to do was switch to classical music."

"Well, clearly she and your father are in this thing together," I explained. "Parents do that all the time."

"Not mine," Kimmy replied. "They're divorced, and they don't speak to each other."

"Oh," I said again, feeling increasingly stupid.

"They have joint custody of me. I go from one big ole ugly mansion to another. Most of the time they don't even know whose house I'm in." She gave me a tortured look.

"That stinks," I said in a low voice.

"I love playing rock and country," Kimmy continued earnestly. "I can't give it up. Next to Savy, it's the best friend I have." She turned her huge myopic blue eyes on Savy. "Well, now maybe it's the *only* friend I have."

"Lord, girl, you should be the Low Self-Esteem Poster Child," Sandra opined, rolling her eyes.

"Kimmy, of course you're my best friend," Savy insisted, grabbing Kimmy's hand. "How can you even say that?"

Kimmy shrugged her already hunched-over shoulders. "You don't hang out with me anymore."

"I'm just busy!" Savy protested. "And every time we invite you to come out with us, you turn us down!"

"Well, I'd be in the way—" Kimmy began.

Sandra whirled around in the front seat and faced her. "Kimmy! Get a grip! This is not National Feel Sorry for Kimmy Day, okay?"

"I'm sorry—" Kimmy apologized.

"Aghhhhh!" Sandra screamed in frustration, smacking herself in the forehead.

"Kimmy, I really, really need you to come through for me now," Savy said in a plaintive voice. "This is the first time a student has been allowed to be musical director. I really want to impress everyone. But without a guitar player, the band is going to sound awful. Please. Do this for me."

"Do this for yourself," Sandra added sharply. "Show a little gumption for once!"

We all waited silently. A bell rang in the school signaling last period.

"Oh, God," Kimmy moaned, screwing her eyes shut tight. She opened them and looked at Savy. "Okay," she finally said. "I'll do it."

Savy hugged Kimmy hard. "Oh, thank you, you won't regret it!"

"I do already," Kimmy replied anxiously.

"Dang, we've got a ton and a half of work to do," Savy said. "We'll have to rehearse tonight at my house, okay? Seven?"

"Since we already missed school, why don't we start now?" Sandra suggested. "Unless one of you wants to run in to school and try to explain where we've been."

"Not me," Kimmy said with a shudder. "This is the very first time I ever cut school in my life."

"Welcome to the wonderful world of sin," Sandra tossed off.

"I've got to go home first and call the girls from the car accident," I reminded them. "And face my mother."

"So, we'll go with you," Savy suggested. "Then she'll have to spring you afterward, right?"

"You don't know my mother," I told her. "All four of us may end up getting locked in my room."

Sandra started up the Jeep, and we headed for my apartment to face the music.

CHAPTER
12

❤

Well, there was good news and there was bad news.

The good news was, the two girls Wyatt hit were both going to be okay. And neither of them was mad at me; they were mad at Wyatt. In fact, the parents of the girl who had broken her collarbone and leg were filing a lawsuit against him. Good.

The bad news was, my mother was so angry that she just about gave birth. I mean, the woman turned every shade of purple. As I said, she *loved* that car. She also could not believe how, as she put it, "incredibly irresponsible, unthinking, and immature" I had been. What could I say? I knew I had messed up in a major way and a lot of people were suffering the consequences.

Oh, yeah, more good news. Mom's insurance company would pay to have her car fixed, and we are talking major dinero here. And her insurance company was going to sue Wyatt, too. Good again.

Although my mom didn't want to let me go to Savy's to band practice, I reminded her that she had already said I could go. She insisted I had to be home at seven for dinner, which I promised, and then I slipped out the door with my friends before she could figure out a way to force me to stay home.

We stopped at Sandra's house to get her bass guitar. She lived near me, it turned out, in an immaculate gray shingled house with the most perfectly trimmed shrubbery and the most perfect, gorgeous flower beds I'd ever seen.

"Who's the gardener?" I asked Sandra.

"My dad," she replied. "He loves working in the garden, he says it relaxes him. But trust me, my dad is an accountant, and he's never relaxed."

"So that's where you get it from," Savy teased her.

"Well, my mom is a session singer," Sandra said. "And she's so laid back she's practically catatonic, so between the two I'm better off taking after my father. Be right back."

"Her mom's a singer, huh?" I asked Savy and Kimmy while we waited for Sandra.

"She sings backup for everybody—Dolly Parton, Garth Brooks—and she does a lot of demo work," Savy said.

"Wait a minute," I said. "She's black and she sings country?"

Savy grinned at me. "I hate to burst your little bubble," she replied, "but it happens."

Sandra came back quickly, and we drove to Kimmy's mother's house to pick up her guitar.

No, not house. Mansion. Estate. Like that.

"How rich *are* your parents?" I asked, as Sandra drove past the fortress-like electric iron gate that surrounded the property and up the endless private road off to Old Hickory Boulevard which led to the house.

"Pretty rich," Kimmy admitted softly, blushing with embarrassment. "My mother is head of the Carrier Foundation. It's a family trust that makes charitable donations to the arts."

"You mean that's, like, her *job?*" I asked derisively, staring out at the massive trees, the manmade lake, and the sweeping hills that made up her—get this—front lawn.

"She works really hard at it," Kimmy said defensively.

So then we came to a private gate. I'm not

kidding. And at this gate was a guardhouse. And a guard. In a uniform.

Kimmy stuck her head out the window. "Hi, Al, it's me," she called.

Al the guard tipped his hat and hit a buzzer in his little guardhouse, and the gate opened.

"Didn't I see this on 'Lifestyles of the Rich and Incredibly Self-Indulgent'?" Sandra wondered as we drove past the guardhouse.

"It's not Kimmy," Savy pointed out. "It's Kimmy's parents."

We came up to the house, a huge, palatial thing with gold filigreed columns and mammoth picture windows letting in the panoramic view. It screamed old money. It made Savy's house look like a shack in comparison.

"I'll just run in and be right back," Kimmy promised, jumping out of the back of the Jeep.

"How does she even find her way around in there when she 'runs in'?" Sandra wondered. "You think she leaves a trail of bread crumbs to find her way back out again?"

"How rich is she, really?" I asked Savy while we waited for Kimmy.

"Real," Savy replied. "But she doesn't like people to know. It embarrasses her. And her parents are just awful. Do you know they won't buy her a car because they tell her the chauffeur can take her wherever she wants to go?"

"You're kidding," Sandra said.

"Nope," Savy replied. "A chauffeur drives her to school and picks her up. Kimmy makes him stop on a side street, and she walks the rest of the way."

"Unreal," I breathed.

"It's partly for security, too," Savy continued. "When Kimmy's older brother, Jason, was six years old, he was kidnapped and held for ransom."

"Somebody told me about that," Sandra put in, "but I didn't believe it was true. It happened before we moved here from Detroit."

"Oh, it's true," Savy confirmed. "They got Jason back, and they caught the kidnappers, but that's why Kimmy's parents are so overprotective of her. They want to know where she is every minute. It's really awful."

"That's why she carries the beeper!" I realized, remembering the beeper that had gone off in her purse when she was at my house. "I thought maybe she was a drug dealer or something!"

"Kimmy?" Savy said with a laugh.

"The girl is afraid of her own shadow," Sandra said. "The only drug she could deal is baby aspirin."

In no time at all Kimmy ran back out with her guitar, jumped in the back seat, and we headed for Savy's house.

"Well, howdy," Gramma Beth said when we all tramped into the house. She was in the front room, going through wallpaper samples. "I didn't expect to see y'all. Which paper do you like for the great room, girls?"

We dutifully looked at her wallpaper samples.

"I thought the paper with the guitars on it was going up," I said, remembering that it half covered some other wallpaper.

"Well, could be," Gramma Beth agreed, "but then again, maybe not. I can never tell for sure until I see it on the wall."

"We have to go practice," Savy told her grandmother. "Wyatt broke his arm, and Kimmy is going to be replacing him in the pit band."

"Well, Lord have mercy!" Gramma Beth boomed, jumping up to hug Kimmy hard. "This means we're all finally going to get to hear you play!"

"Unless I fall over in a dead faint, which is a really strong possibility," Kimmy replied in a tremulous voice.

"Oh, shoot, ain't nothin' to it but to do it. I've been tellin' you that for years," Gramma Beth told Kimmy. "Why don't I get you girls a snack for your break?" She gave Kimmy another hug. "I'm proud of you, girl!"

We quickly set up our stuff in the music room while Kimmy looked over the score to *Grease*.

"What do you think?" Sandra asked her.

"I don't know," Kimmy said meekly.

"Can you play it or not?" Sandra asked impatiently.

"I'm not sure," Kimmy faltered.

"Well, dress rehearsal is tomorrow night so you need to *get* sure," I snapped. Kimmy's insecurity was really starting to annoy me.

"You can play it, Kimmy, I know you can," Savy said earnestly.

"Maybe y'all should ask someone from a different school," Kimmy suggested. "We could call over to Hillsboro High—"

"Let's just try a song before you replace yourself," Savy said. "How about 'Worse Things,' Rizzo's ballad."

"I'll try," Kimmy whispered, blowing a wisp of her blond hair out of her eyes.

"Great," Sandra muttered sarcastically.

Savy counted us off, and we started playing the song. The guitar part was straight-ahead; the song was slow and not too musically difficult. Kimmy played tentatively, but she hit the right notes most of the time.

"That was fine!" Savy cried, hugging Kimmy. "See, I knew you could do it!"

Sandra and I traded looks. *That* was the great guitar playing Savy had bragged about? It was barely competent. However, we needed Kimmy. Building her up seemed like the best thing to do.

"Yeah, you hung right in there," I said, trying to sound enthusiastic.

"I did?" Kimmy asked, biting her lower lip.

"Absolutely," I told her.

"Let's try 'Magic Changes,' " Savy suggested. "It's a rocker, but it's pretty basic."

We turned to the rock song that Doody sings in Act One when he imagines himself to be a rock star.

"You start it off, Kimmy," Savy pointed out.

Kimmy nodded and began to play—C, F minor, A, G—simple chords. We all came in on our parts. But then, in mid-song, it started to cook. I looked over at Kimmy. She was playing more confidently, adding a little riff of her own. Then another. Then another.

Oh, my God, she was good. She was really, really good.

"Get down!" Sandra cheered when we finished playing the song. "You really *can* play!"

"I can?" Kimmy asked, a grin spreading across her face.

"Yes, yes, a thousand times yes!" Savy cried. "I want to do 'All Shook Up.' It really rocks."

We turned to the big rock duet between Danny and Sandy at the end of the show. Savy counted us in, and we all began to play. Now Kimmy went even further, and she was incredible! She was better than Wyatt! She might even have been better than Chad!

When we finished the tune, Savy, Sandra, and I started jumping around the room, screaming with excitement.

"Holy sugar on a shingle!" I screamed, grabbing Kimmy and whirling her around in a circle. "You are unbelievable!"

Kimmy laughed one of the happiest laughs I've ever heard. "I can do even better after I've played it a few times," she told me eagerly.

"Let's do that one again!" Savy suggested. "Just rock out on that solo part, okay?"

"Okay," Kimmy agreed, pulling the strap of her guitar back over her shoulder.

We played the song again, and Kimmy really did play it even better. She was hot, original, unbelievable!

Somewhere during the song Gramma Beth came to the doorway with a tray of iced tea and cookies. She set the tray down and stood there watching us. When we finished she walked over to Kimmy and took her by the shoulders. "Child, I am so proud of you." She gave Kimmy a huge hug.

"I really can play?" Kimmy asked, searching Gramma Beth's face for the truth. "Y'all aren't just saying that to make me feel good?"

"Oh, shoot, Kimmy, you know me better than

that," Gramma Beth scolded. "You have a gift, which means you have to work hard. It's a sin to turn your back on a gift like that."

We ate all the cookies on the tray, and then we played for hours, going through the score three times. I had the greatest time. When I remembered to look at my watch it was six forty-five.

"I gotta motor or my mother will kill me," I told them. "Listen, this was unbelievably cool."

"How about if we practice again tomorrow after school?" Savy suggested. "Then we'll know we'll be ready for the dress rehearsal tomorrow night."

Kimmy's face paled. "Oh, God," she moaned. "I can't do this in front of people!"

"You can!" Savy insisted. "I know you can!"

"Sure you can," Sandra agreed. "Try this. Whenever I'm scared of something, I just say to myself, 'What's the worst thing that could happen?' It's never that bad!"

"I could faint," Kimmy worried. "I could throw up in front of the whole school. I could throw up and *then* faint in front of the whole school—"

"On second thought, scratch that concept from your character-building repertoire," Sandra suggested wryly.

"Hi, Jane!" Timmy called, walking on stiff legs into the music room.

"Hi," I replied with a grin, happy to see him out of his wheelchair.

"Want to stay for dinner?" he asked me hopefully.

"Sorry, big guy, I can't," I told him. "But I'll be back over tomorrow."

"Oh, cool," he said, striving for a nonchalance that he obviously didn't feel. Savy had confided that Timmy had been writing me a love ballad.

Sandra, Kimmy, and I went out to Sandra's Jeep and drove back to my apartment.

"Listen, you guys, I really want to thank you for . . . well, for everything," I told them.

Sandra shrugged coolly, and Kimmy just pushed her glasses up her nose.

Huh.

Well, who knew why they had helped me out? I certainly didn't. Kimmy was jealous because she thought I was stealing away her best friend, and Sandra was so cool and played things so close to the vest it was impossible to know *what* she really thought. I mean, the only one who I felt sure really liked me was Savy. But then, Savy liked everybody. Anyway, they had saved my butt, and I was truly grateful.

Still, in my heart of hearts, it would have been nicer to know they did it because they really, truly liked me.

Not that I'd ever admit that.

CHAPTER
13

♡

Up to this point Jill hadn't said a word to me about my big scandal, but the next morning she kept staring at me as we got dressed for school, like she was worried she might be sharing a room with a serial killer.

"What?" I finally exploded.

"Mom and Dad told me what happened," she said significantly.

"And?" I asked her in a bored voice.

"And everyone at my school is talking about you," she added.

"Yeah, and I care what the chatter is at Green Hills Middle School." I pulled my black jeans out of my drawer and wriggled into them. Then I pulled on a black turtleneck and looked at myself in the mirror. Very fifties beatnik. Good. I wanted to look mysterious, unshakable, untouchable. I figured everyone at school would be gossiping about me even more than usual. I wanted to look aloof from it all, impervious to their whispers and digs. I perched a black beret on my head at an angle.

"Oh, I know you don't care," Jill said, putting some tasteful little pearl studs into her pierced ears. "You don't care about anything or anybody except yourself. I can't believe Mom and Dad didn't punish you even more than they did."

I stared at my little sister, now clad in a sunny yellow skirt and sweater set with, natch, a matching hair bow. I definitely detected a trace of southern drawl in her speech. "Were you always this much of a suck-up, or has it gotten worse since you turned into Scarlett O'Hara?"

"Billy Bob says Katie Lynn told him Wyatt only went out with you because you begged him to," Jill informed me.

"Do tell," I muttered, searching through my drawer for my darkest sunglasses to complete my outfit. "And what else did Katie Lynn lie about?"

"Billy said Katie took some homemade cookies over to Wyatt's last night as a get-well present, and Wyatt told Katie you were drunk and the two of you Did It in the back of Mom's car."

I slammed the drawer shut and spun around. "And what did you say?"

"I said I was pretty sure you were adopted."

Wow, that hurt. I couldn't believe how much that hurt.

"Thanks, Jill," I said in a low voice. "Thanks a lot."

"Well, you brought this on yourself!" Jill cried defensively. "It's not my fault, it's your own!"

I found my dark glasses and put them on. I didn't care. I was cool, decadent, an existential beatnik from another generation, and I didn't care about anything or anyone.

School sucked.

From the way the pastel people acted, you would have thought I'd been on "America's Most Wanted" the night before. Whenever I walked into a room, everyone would fall silent; then they'd all start whispering again. I kept my sunglasses on and told all my teachers it was because I had a sty.

I hoped lunchtime would offer me a brief reprieve from my leper status, but Savy was meeting with Ms. Jacobi about the dress rehearsal, so she wasn't in the cafeteria. Sandra was there, but she was sitting with some friends from the African American Student Union across the room, and she just nodded coolly at me. I picked up a chicken salad sandwich in the food line and sat down with Kimmy. Not a good idea. If anything she was more upset than I was. She moaned on and on about how she just couldn't play in the band, how she felt sick, et cetera, et cetera. I finally left and took a walk around the school just to get away from her.

Somehow I made it through my afternoon classes. It wasn't easy. All too often I overheard snatches of what the pastel people were saying about me: She got drunk and Did It with Wyatt. She Did It with Wyatt's entire band. She Did It with every guy at the party. And then I would hear them quacking—they made sure I heard that. What a slut, they were saying. If she walks like a duck and talks like a duck ...

Quack-quack-quack.

I remembered once, a long time ago, I was upset about not getting picked for a club at school that I wanted to be in, and I cried to my mother that it wasn't fair. And I remember my mom said to me, with the saddest look in her eyes, "Honey, the world isn't fair." Those words came back to me when I heard that hideous quack-quack-quack as I walked down the hall. I was being labeled a slut and accused of doing things I had never done.

My mom was right. The world was not fair.

We planned to meet Sandra at her Jeep right

after school and go to Savy's for a final practice before the dress rehearsal that night.

I got to the Jeep first and was leaning against it, my eyes closed behind my dark glasses, taking in the afternoon sun, when I heard the ugly quack-quack-quack of some pastel people going by.

I opened my eyes and then shut them again.

Sandra walked over to me. "Does that bother you?" she asked me.

"Please," I scoffed.

She gave me an appraising look and opened the Jeep. I wanted to tell her the truth—that they were making up lies about me, that none of the rumors about me were true except that I'd been at the party and Wyatt had driven my mom's car. But I clenched my fists and kept my mouth shut. I was not going to care. I refused to care.

Savy and Kimmy showed up a few minutes later.

"I cleared everything with Ms. Jacobi, about Kimmy playing instead of Wyatt," Savy told us as we all piled into the Jeep. "She was a little surprised, since she never even knew Kimmy played guitar."

"Did you tell her how good Kimmy is?" I asked Savy.

"I'm not," Kimmy protested softly, as if all our encouragement of her talent the day before had never happened.

Although Kimmy always dressed in baggy nondescript clothes, today she had outdone herself in the please-don't-notice-me-wardrobe department. She had on a brown sweater that was at least four sizes too big and a beige skirt that hung in baggy folds to her calves. Her hair was pulled straight back with a barrette. She bit her lip and was biting her nails down to the nubs.

"I told her you were good," Savy replied, looking at Kimmy. "I figured this way she'll be happily surprised when it turns out you're great."

"Oh, God," Kimmy groaned, sliding down the seat. "I feel sick."

"If you hurl in my Jeep you're gonna feel a lot sicker," Sandra warned Kimmy as she pulled out of the parking lot.

Sandra pushed a tape into her tape player and the sound of Garth Brooks singing a gospel-sounding tune called "We Shall Be Free" filled the Jeep. I listened to the lyrics. Way cool.

"Hey, I thought Garth Brooks only sang country," I said to Sandra.

"That *is* country," Sandra replied, stopping at a light.

"No way," I protested. "It's gospel with kind of a funk backbeat."

Sandra smiled. "It's also country. My mom is singing backup."

"For real?" I asked, and turned the tape up louder. "It sounds great."

"My mother is a great singer," Sandra agreed. "You ever hear the song 'Hopeless'? That's my mom doing all the backup solos."

"And Garth sings the hell out of it," Sandra said. She rummaged around in her tapes, popped out that tape, and put in another. Sure enough, it was Garth Brooks singing Billy Joel's song. And he sounded hot. So did Sandra's mom.

"So, was your mom a session singer when you lived in Detroit?" I asked Sandra.

"Yep," Sandra replied, "only once Motown left and rap and hip-hop took over, there wasn't enough work for her, so we moved here."

Sandra's mom took a soaring riff solo on the tape.

"Wow, she's great," I told Sandra.

Sandra smiled. "I know." She pulled her Jeep into Savy's driveway.

Kimmy ran in first to use the bathroom.

"Is she going to be able to handle this?" I asked Savy.

"I hope so" was Savy's not very encouraging response. Sandra just rolled her eyes with impatience.

We went to the music room and started warming up, waiting for Kimmy. Finally she showed up, looking pale and drawn.

"You okay?" Savy asked her.

She nodded mutely and picked up her guitar.

"Okay, let's run through the whole score from the beginning," Savy said. "I'll sing the lead vocals so you can get the gist of how it'll sound tonight."

We began with the high school anthem that opened the show, which was musically very simple, and Kimmy did fine. By the time we got to "Tell Me More," the first song that the Pink Ladies and the Burger Palace Boys sang together, Kimmy seemed much more relaxed. The longer we played, the better she got. We cruised into the last number in Act One and finished big.

"Great!" Savy cried, spinning around on her piano bench.

"You're fine once you get into it," I told Kimmy.

"Ever hear the saying 'There is nothing to fear but fear itself'?" Sandra asked her.

"Franklin Delano Roosevelt," Kimmy said, nodding. "I do know that . . . in theory, anyway."

We took a five-minute break and then tackled the second act. Now Kimmy was much more relaxed and confident. She played even better than she had the day before. We cruised through the score, no problem. Kimmy even started to loosen up physically. Her hair came out of the barrette,

and her shoulders weren't hunched over anymore. I thought again how pretty she was, especially now, with her face shining and her blond
hair whirling around her face. The change was
kinda astonishing, really.

When we got to the big finish, Kimmy really let
loose and wailed. That inspired me—it seemed to
inspire all of us—and we brought it home with a
flourish.

"Well, get down, girl!" Sandra cried when we
finished.

Kimmy grinned at us, shy and happy at the
same time.

Sandra began to dance around, playing the
bass line to the rock classic "Gloria" by Van
Morrison. Kimmy recognized the riff and came
in on guitar. I joined in on drums, and Savy came
in on piano. Savy began singing the verse, and
on the chorus we all came in together. It seemed
natural to fall into harmony, and we did, rocking
out together.

"Hey, do y'all know Jerry Lee Lewis's 'Great
Balls of Fire'?" Savy asked us. We all did, and
played it while Savy sang. Again we all came in
on the chorus in harmony. It was great fun, and
we sounded . . . well, we sounded really good!

As for Kimmy, she seemed like an entirely different girl. She was grinning, confident, dancing

around with her guitar. All her self-consciousness seemed to have fallen away. It was just incredible.

When we finished the tune, I heard clapping and whistling, and I looked up to see Gramma Beth in the doorway. The dozens of bangle bracelets on her arms jingled and clinked together musically.

"Well, hog-tie me to a tadpole, you girls can play!" Gramma Beth cried happily.

"Come on and play with us," Savy begged her grandmother.

"Much as I'd love to, I've got to go give a fiddle lesson," Gramma Beth said. "Kimmy Carrier, you are a hellified guitar player!"

"Oh, I don't know . . ." Kimmy protested.

"That is no way to take a heartfelt compliment," Gramma Beth chided. "You say thank you."

Kimmy ducked her head down into her shoulders.

"Just open your mouth and say it!" Gramma Beth instructed Kimmy. "Thank. You."

"Thank you," Kimmy finally said meekly.

"There, wasn't so hard, was it?" Gramma Beth said with a huge grin. "I can't wait to hear y'all at the play tomorrow night. It's really gonna be something special." She walked over and gave her granddaughter a hug.

"Thanks, Gramma," Savy said.

"You know, I was watching you girls from the doorway," Gramma Beth continued, looking at

Savy, "and I remembered how you always told me you wanted your own band. From the time you were a bitty little thing that's what you always told me. And I was watching you girls and I thought, 'Dang, if Savy doesn't have what she's always wanted!' "

"Well, I have my own band for the four nights of the school play, anyway," Savy said with a laugh.

"You girls sound mighty good together," Gramma Beth insisted. "And you look good together, too. There's no reason in the world you couldn't be a band if you wanted to." She kissed Savy on the forehead. "Well, I gotta run and teach this kid who has no musical ability whatsoever."

"Maybe you should just tell the kid's parents that, so they don't waste their money," Sandra said loftily.

"I have," Gramma Beth responded. "But the child loves to play anyway, so I guess even the talentless have the right to make music in this world. Bye, girls!"

"Your grandmother is, as my mother the aging hippie would say, a trip," Sandra said wryly.

Savy was looking pensively into the distance. "Maybe she's right," she muttered.

"What?" Kimmy asked, slicking her hair back into her barrette.

"Maybe . . . maybe it's not crazy," Savy said to the air.

"Earth to Savy," I called. "Are you planet-hopping again?"

Savy cocked her head in my direction. "Maybe . . . well, why couldn't we be a band? Why couldn't we actually be a band?"

It was quiet in the room.

"You mean like a play-music-together-in-public kind of band?" Kimmy asked, aghast.

"No, she means a secret band that no one knows about," I replied.

"A country-rock band," Savy continued earnestly, ignoring Kimmy. "We're really good together, and we haven't even practiced very much. Just think what we could do!"

Kimmy blushed. "I just meant, you know, I never could do something like that."

"And I'm too busy," Sandra added with a shrug.

"And I could never be in a band unless it was a really serious band, which clearly this isn't," I said.

Savy walked over to me, her eyes shining. "But it could be! You know I'm a serious musician!"

"But I hate country music!" I protested.

"You just *think* you hate country," Sandra said. "You didn't hate those Garth tunes I played in the Jeep, did you?"

"Well, no," I allowed, "but that's not—"

"That's country!" Kimmy, Savy, and Sandra all said together.

I looked from one of them to the other. "Okay, that's country. Goody. We still aren't gonna be a band, so it's a moot point, right?"

"Right," Sandra agreed.

Savy's face fell.

"Savy, I am number one in our class, and I intend to stay there," Sandra said tersely. "I teach aerobics, I'm captain of the tennis team and president of the junior class—I haven't got time to be in a band."

"It wouldn't have to take all that much time," Savy protested.

"It would if it was going to be any good," Sandra pointed out, "and if it wasn't going to be first rate I wouldn't want to be in it anyway."

"That's what you call your basic catch-22," I pointed out.

"Yeah, I guess," Savy finally said reluctantly. She sat back down on her piano bench, looking more crestfallen than I'd ever seen her. "It's just that it could be so fantastic. . . ."

It really could. That's what I was thinking to myself. I missed the Chill so much, and Savy, Sandra, Kimmy, and I really *were* great together.

But as long as Kimmy was afraid of her own shadow and Sandra was busy being Miss Everything, there was no way we could ever be a band.

Besides, I hated country music.

CHAPTER 14

"Jane, we need to have a serious talk."

Thus spoke my mother, standing in the doorway of my room. My father stood next to her with his arms folded in his best no-nonsense pose.

It was the next night, a half hour before I was supposed to leave to meet the band for warm-up before the opening night of *Grease*. The dress rehearsal had gone great. Once Kimmy realized that the kids in the play were more worried about their own parts than they were about hers, she did fine. Oh, a few people gawked and whispered—they couldn't believe Kimmy Carrier could play guitar like that—but most kids in the play were cut from cooler cloth than the pastel people, and they were more interested in a great production than they were fascinated by Kimmy's talent or my scandal.

Kimmy had finished rehearsal the night before on an up note. Ms. Jacobi had been incredibly impressed with Kimmy's talent and had told her so. Tonight would tell the tale, though. Two hundred people would be watching Kimmy play. Whether or not she could do it without falling apart remained to be seen. And if she did fall apart and the play was ruined, it seemed to me that it would be my fault. I mean, Kimmy hadn't wanted to do it; she was only playing because of Wyatt's broken arm. And if I hadn't met Wyatt at that stupid party and let him drive when he'd been drinking, he'd still be in the band. Secretly, in my heart of hearts, that was how I looked at it. I blamed myself, which made me feel anxious, nervous, crazed.

And now Mom and Dad had picked this auspicious moment to tell me we needed to have a serious talk. Great timing.

"Okay," I agreed reluctantly, dropping an oversized peace symbol around my neck.

Like I actually had a choice.

"Let's go into the living room," my mother suggested.

"Sandra is picking me up in ten minutes," I reminded them as we walked into the living room.

"Well, this won't take long," my mother said, taking a seat on the couch with my father. They were both dressed up for the play, my dad in an ill-fitting suit and my mom in a hideous polka-dot dress with a fitted waist and a little matching jacket. Jill was at her friend Tara's house—I'm not kidding; the girl was actually named Tara—and was coming to the play with Tara's family.

"You guys look nice," I told them. This was designed to soften them up. Not that they weren't presentable, but neither of them had the fashion sense of a gerbil.

"You know we agreed you could be in the band for this play," my mother said, ignoring my compliment, "and we're sure you're going to be wonderful."

I smiled noncommittally, because I knew now my mother was trying to soften *me* up. That meant something really, really bad was coming.

"But in a few days the play will be over, and we need to discuss the situation with my car," my mother continued.

"We received a letter from our insurance carrier today," my father said. "Because of the accident with your mother's car, they're raising our insurance premiums by a thousand dollars."

"A thousand dollars?" I repeated, feeling faint. They both nodded.

"We consider that thousand-dollar increase your responsibility," my father said.

"You do?" I asked.

They nodded together again, two little parent-puppets.

How do parents learn how to do this stuff? I mean, they don't train for their positions. But my parents were killers at presenting your basic United Front. They were unshakable. No way could I divide and conquer.

No way out, no way out.

"I have a little money in my savings account," I began.

"Very little," my mother pointed out.

She was right, of course. Seventy-nine dollars and fifty cents, the last time I looked.

"So, we'd like your input on how you can be responsible for this thousand dollars," my father said.

Sha, right. As if.

This was sort of like the family-vote things we did. It didn't matter how I voted then, and it didn't matter what I said now. Basically they were telling me: you are screwed.

"Uh, you want me to get a part-time job?" I asked them.

"What do you think?" my father asked.

Like he cared. On the other hand, they were right. That thousand-dollar increase *was* my fault.

"Well, when your car is fixed and I have my car back, I'll go to the mall and look for a part-time job, okay?" I asked them.

"Then you agree that this is your responsibility," my mother said.

"What if I didn't agree? It wouldn't matter," I said.

"Jane—" my father began.

"I'm not saying you're not right," I continued. "I just hate it when you pretend that I have input in this family when I don't." I got up and looked out the window. I saw Sandra's Jeep turning down our street. "I have to go."

"We'll be discussing this further," my father said.

"You're the boss, boss," I pointed out, and headed out the door.

"Hi," Sandra said when I got into her Jeep. "You look nice."

"I look just like you," I said with a laugh.

We were both wearing black jeans and white tuxedo shirts that Ms. Jacobi had purchased for the band.

Sandra drove to Kimmy's, where both Savy and Kimmy were waiting. They both looked very cute in their jeans and tux shirts. Kimmy, with her long, lean frame and blond hair would probably have looked the best of all of us, if her face hadn't been as white as her tux shirt.

Kimmy and Savy climbed into the Jeep. Kimmy sat in the back and stared out the window as if she were a zombie.

"How you doing?" I asked Kimmy.

She stared out the window as if she hadn't heard me.

"How long has this been going on?" I asked Savy.

"A couple of hours," Savy said. "Kimmy's mother came to her room to tell her she wasn't coming to the play because she couldn't possibly sit through it."

"Gee, nice," I commented.

"Is her dad coming?" Sandra asked.

"No," Savy said. "He told Kimmy when she comes to her senses and stops wasting whatever talent she has, he'll be ready to listen."

"Except I don't have any talent," Kimmy said, still staring out the window.

"Here we go again," Sandra groaned from the front seat.

"Listen, Kimmy, they're wrong," I told her firmly.

She didn't respond.

Savy shrugged and made a praying gesture with her hands, looking up at the roof of the car.

Sandra parked in the school parking lot, and Savy led Kimmy-the-Zombie into the auditorium. Kids were running around, screaming, laughing, checking lights and props. We propelled Kimmy into the pit so we could warm up.

Kimmy just stood there. Savy picked up Kimmy's guitar and gently handed it to her.

"Hi, girls!" Ms. Jacobi called, walking briskly into the auditorium. "You look great!"

"Thanks," Savy managed, tearing her eyes away from Kimmy, who was just standing there holding the guitar, staring at the floor.

"Is she okay?" Ms. Jacobi asked, eyeing Kimmy with concern.

"Oh, sure," Sandra replied breezily. "She's just . . . concentrating."

"Oh," the teacher said, still eyeing Kimmy. "Well, let me know if you guys need anything, okay?"

"Sure," Savy said.

Ms. Jacobi smiled and walked off.

"Kimmy, we're going to run through 'All Choked Up,' okay?" Savy asked.

Nothing.

"Kimmy?" Savy touched her arm, and Kimmy jumped as if she'd been hit by lightning.

"What?" she gasped.

" 'All Choked Up'?" Savy repeated.

Savy led us in, and we played the tune. Kimmy was behind on the beat. She messed up her solo. She played the wrong chord a few times. Every time she made a mistake, her playing got worse.

"I can't do this!" Kimmy cried, stopping in the middle of the song. "I'm ruining everything!"

"That's right," Sandra agreed, clearly pissed off, "so snap out of it!"

Savy reached over and grabbed Kimmy's arm. "You *can* do this!"

"I can't!" Kimmy cried.

"Let's just try a different song," Savy suggested. "You just need time to warm up. Let's do 'Greased Lightning.' "

This was a hot rocker that the boys in the Burger Palace sang about a souped-up car. Kimmy played as if she had recently learned a few chords. It was a disaster. We limped our way through it and ended with Kimmy playing the wrong chord.

Silence.

"That was awful!" the stage manager said, standing in the wings. "What happened? You sounded great yesterday!"

"And we'll sound great tonight," Savy assured him. "We're just warming up."

"Well, you sound pretty danged cold right now," the stage manager muttered and wandered off with his clipboard.

"Oh, God, oh, God, oh, God," Kimmy moaned, burying her head in her hands.

"Hey, I'm opening the house in five minutes,"

a thin girl called from the back of the auditorium. "Y'all need to clear out."

Savy helped Kimmy out of the pit, and the four of us walked silently down the hall to the music room where we had jazz band practice. We sat Kimmy in a chair, and then the three of us huddled together in the hall outside the door.

"We are totally screwed," I stated.

"I cannot believe that girl," Sandra said with disgust. "She has no backbone."

"Try to understand," Savy said earnestly. "She's scared out of her mind."

"Oh, please," Sandra scoffed testily. "Being broke and homeless with five kids is being scared out of your mind. A rich girl who freaks out over the school play doesn't qualify."

I looked over at Sandra. "Have you ever been broke or homeless?"

"No," Sandra admitted.

"Have you ever been so scared that you were literally paralyzed and couldn't function, like Kimmy is right now?"

"No," Sandra said.

"So you really don't know about it either way, do you," I stated.

"Hey, I—" Sandra began.

"Look, fighting among ourselves is not going to solve this problem," Savy interrupted, holding her hands up to both of us. "I think the best thing we can do is go into that room and tell Kimmy that we have all the faith in the world in her. Then we pray as hard as we can."

Sandra and I both just stared at her.

"You ready?" Savy asked us.

"Ready," Sandra allowed. "I just hope this works."

We walked back into the music room.

"I am so sorry," Kimmy whispered to us, her glasses in her hand. Her face was streaked with tears.

"Look, it's not important," Savy insisted gently, pulling a seat up next to Kimmy. "There's some saying about when you have a bad warm-up it means you're going to have a great show."

"I . . . I just kept hearing my mother's voice in my head, you know?" Kimmy said earnestly. " 'You have no talent. You can't do it.' "

"But we know you can," I said firmly. "We heard you play that score great."

More tears slid down Kimmy's face. "Y'all can't imagine how awful this feels, to be this scared."

"Bull," Sandra said.

Kimmy turned her huge blue eyes at Sandra.

"What makes you think none of us know what it's like to be scared?" Sandra asked.

"You can't know," Kimmy insisted. "I always feel . . . out of it, different, a loser."

"Everyone feels like that sometimes," Savy said.

Kimmy shook her head. "Not the three of you," she said, blowing her nose noisily with a Kleenex. "The three of you are the most confident people I know. Especially you," she added, jutting her chin toward Sandra.

"You think it's easy being black at Green Hills High?" Sandra asked Kimmy.

"Well, no," Kimmy allowed, "I guess it isn't."

"You think it's easy being Jewish in the Bible Belt?" Savy asked.

"Maybe not," Kimmy said, "but being black or being Jewish means at least you belong somewhere!"

"So what about me?" I finally asked Kimmy. "Where the hell do *I* belong?"

Kimmy stared at me. "I don't know," she finally said. "But you're so tough you don't care."

I gulped hard. I could tell the truth or I could hide.

"Want to know how many times I've cried myself to sleep since we moved to Nashville?" I asked Kimmy.

Everyone stared at me.

"I was so afraid people wouldn't like me that I acted as obnoxious and as weird as I could, just to make them think I didn't care. I even went out with that dirtbag, Wyatt, because I wanted to prove how cool I am."

I could feel hot tears threatening my eyes, but I willed them down. "Now all those mental midgets at school think I'm some kind of a slut, and I walk down the hall and hear them quacking at me, and I pretend I don't care, that it doesn't hurt . . ."

A tear slid down my cheek. I couldn't stop it.

"But it does hurt," I managed, my voice going squeaky. "It hurts a lot. I didn't have sex with Wyatt. I haven't had sex with anyone yet. I don't know if I'll ever fit in here. And I miss my friends and my life in New York so much that sometimes I just want to die."

There was a knock on the door, and Ms. Jacobi stuck her head in. "We need you girls in the pit," she said. "The show is starting in five minutes."

So. Did you ever hear that saying, "Confession is good for the soul"? What a crock. I didn't feel a bit better. The only difference was, now three other people knew about it.

And I didn't have any time to find out if my gut-wrenching saga had had any effect on Kimmy, because we had to rush to the stage and down into the pit. No one said a word to me. I hoped it was because they were all still too busy worrying about whether Kimmy was even going to be able to actually play the guitar that Savy placed in her trembling hands. On the other hand, it was certainly possible that no one had said anything to me because I had just made a total fool out of myself.

There's nothing quite as awful as sticking your heart out there in the road for people to run over.

My eyes were just at the level where I could raise my head and see into the auditorium. I couldn't see one empty seat. The crowd buzzed with anticipation. The house lights dimmed.

Without a word Savy reached over and took my hand. I reached over for Sandra, and Sandra reached out to Kimmy. Kimmy took her hand. We looked at one another. Each of us had something big to prove that night, and each of us was dependent on the other three girls whose hands we held at that moment.

It was kinda terrific, and kinda terrifying, both at the same time.

CHAPTER 15

I really, really, really had to pee.

But I forgot about it in an instant when Savy got the cue through her headphones from the stage manager and nodded at us to start the opening song.

So far so good. Kimmy was playing. She was hitting the right notes. Onstage the number broke out into a wild dance. Kimmy kept up. We finished the song right on the money.

Then the audience applauded. All two hundred of them.

I looked over at Kimmy and saw the tiniest smile at the corner of her mouth.

Well, who could blame her? The sound of two hundred people clapping for you is heady stuff.

I grinned back at her and nodded my head slightly. She nodded back at me.

The more we played, the better Kimmy got. The better we all got. By the end of Act One, she was the Kimmy who had dazzled me with her talent at Savy's house. By the end of the show she had gone even further. She was absolutely brilliant. It was one of those rare moments in life when things went even better than I could ever have possibly dreamed. The actors got a standing ovation, and when they gestured to the band and we stood up, the audience applauded even harder and yelled "Bravo!"

As the happy, chattering audience filed out of the auditorium, the four of us hugged each other and jumped up and down with relief and happiness.

"You were incredible!" Savy cried, squeezing Kimmy hard. "I knew you could do it! Your parents are totally wrong! You are so talented!"

"Kimmy?" a male voice said from the stage.

We looked up, and there stood Sawyer Paxton, the secret love of Kimmy's life. He still had on the black leather jacket he'd worn in the last scene of the play.

"Yes?" Kimmy asked him.

"You were great," he told her. "You are really an awesome guitarist."

"Oh, no, I'm not," Kimmy protested, her face

turning bright red. Then she caught Savy's face out of the corner of her eye, and Savy put her hands on her hips, as if to remind her of what Gramma Beth had said about how to accept a heartfelt compliment. Kimmy turned back to Sawyer. "I mean"—she took a huge gulp of air—"thank you."

"So, listen, I still haven't done my new demo, because I've been too busy with the play," Sawyer explained. "Jane said she'd play drums. And I was thinking maybe if you're free we could talk about you playing on the demo?" Sawyer asked Kimmy.

"I . . . I . . ." she stammered.

"Go for it, girl," Sandra urged quietly.

"I'd love to," Kimmy managed.

"Cool," Sawyer said with a grin. "I'll call you." Then he ran backstage.

"Did that really just happen?" Kimmy asked faintly.

"I saw it, I heard it, it happened, and you deserve it," Sandra told her, grinning happily.

"Girls!" Ms. Jacobi called to us. "Come backstage! Everyone wants to congratulate you!"

"Let's go get our well-deserved accolades!" Savy said.

We climbed out of the pit. The other three were ahead of me and had just climbed up onto the stage when I heard a deep female voice from somewhere behind me.

"Hey, which one of you is Jane McVay?"

I turned around. There was the biggest, scariest-looking girl I had ever seen in my life. She had to be almost six feet tall and had to weigh an easy one-sixty, but she wasn't fat; we're talking solid muscle. Her overbleached blond hair was ratted up to make her appear even taller. She had on slashes of black eyeliner and long, pointy fake fingernails that looked as if they could double as a serious weapon. Her black leather miniskirt barely covered her crotch, and underneath her motorcycle jacket she had on a T-shirt decorated with a skull and crossbones.

If it had been a costume, I would have thought it was way cool—you know, sort of Rebel Tough Girl from the Wrong Side of the Tracks—but I had a feeling she dressed this way every day.

"I'm Jane," I said, but only because I couldn't figure out a way to pin the name on anyone else.

"Oh, yeah?" the girl sniggered, looking me over. "Well, I'm Brenda Pirkell, Wyatt Shane's girlfriend."

"Good for you," I said. I glanced up to the stage where Savy, Sandra, and Kimmy were standing and shrugged.

"Look, I know what you did, you little slut," Brenda said. "Wyatt told me all about it."

"I bet," I said sarcastically. In case you think I was being really brave, I wasn't. I just figured she couldn't actually kill me right there in the auditorium with three witnesses.

"Listen, bitch," Brenda continued, taking a menacing step toward me, "because of you he's had to cancel all his gigs for the next two months."

"It's his own fault, not mine," I snapped.

"Oh, yeah, sure," Brenda snorted, "like you weren't begging for him, like you weren't trying to steal him away from me. I ought to kick your ass."

I was ready with a witty comeback, but just at that moment the doors opened in the back of the auditorium, and in walked three girls dressed in variations on Brenda's fashion theme, all of them big, all of them bad, all of them tattooed.

They stood with Brenda and stared me down. Gulp.

"Look, I have nothing to say to you," I told Brenda. I started to turn away, but Brenda grabbed my shoulder and jerked me back around to face her.

"Don't you dare turn your back on me, you rich bitch!" Brenda yelled.

I was pissed. If she was going to deck me, she was going to deck me. I grabbed her hand and flung it off. "Keep your hands off of me, I mean it—"

"Oh, yeah, you gonna make me?" Brenda taunted me, moving in for the kill.

"If I have to," I said in what I hoped was a steely voice. Sometimes my temper gets me into trouble, and I don't let anyone push me around, but the truth was I had never been in a physical fight in my life.

"Right," Brenda snickered, looking over at her three gigunda friends. "You and who else, bitch?"

"Me."

Who said that? I looked behind me, and there, coming down the steps from the stage, was none other than scared-of-her-own-shadow Kimmy Carrier. She stood next to me, folded her arms, and stared Brenda right in the eye. They were about the same height.

"And me," came another voice from the stage.

It was Sandra. She calmly walked down the steps and stood on the other side of me.

"And me," Savy added, quickly joining us.

We stood there, the four of us, staring down those big, bad, tattooed girls.

"You ain't heard the last of this," Brenda finally said. Then she turned around, jerked her head to her friends, and they booked for the back door.

I looked over at Kimmy. "I can't believe you just did that."

"Me, either," she said in a tiny voice. "But something inside me just said 'Kimmy, you have to stand up with Jane,' and so ... I did!"

Savy jumped down into the pit and began pounding a wild rock riff on the piano keys. I recognized it as an old classic, "Wild Thing." She stood up and danced around as she played, like she was Elton John or Billy Joel, and she sang at the top of her lungs, but instead of singing the words "wild thing," she sang "Kim-my"!

As if on cue, Sandra, Kimmy, and I jumped down into the pit and joined in, singing lustily. We rocked out, singing, playing, boogying out. Somehow that song turned into "Eight Days a Week," and then "Blue Suede Shoes," and then we finished with "Hey, Jude," all of us doing "na-na-na-na-na-na-na" for all we were worth.

It was one of the highest, happiest moments of my life. I felt like Sally Field when she won that Oscar years ago, and she looked out at all the people, and she said, "You like me! You really like me!"

We hadn't realized it, but a crowd had gathered. They clapped and whooped and whistled their approval. I could see my parents and Jill in the crowd. For once, Jill actually looked happy that I was her sister.

The Leeman clan ran over and surrounded Savy, hugging her with excitement.

"Girls, you are hot stuff and I'm proud of you!" Gramma Beth cried with delight.

"You were great, Jane," Timmy said, blushing furiously.

"He's right," one of Savy's incredibly cute twin brothers agreed, kissing me on the cheek. "I'm Dustin, by the way," he added, knowing I couldn't tell him from his brother.

"Y'all are quite a band," Savy's dad said, nodding with pride. He kissed his daughter on the forehead. "We'll see you back at the house."

"Y'all, we *are* a band!" Savy cried after her family left. Her eyes were shining. "We can't stop now!"

And somehow, at that moment, we all seemed to know it was true. Kimmy didn't protest that she didn't have any talent, and Sandra didn't bring up how busy she was, and I didn't need to insist it had to be a serious band because that was obvious.

The house manager made the crowd leave the auditorium, telling them we'd meet them in the lobby in a few minutes.

The auditorium was so quiet you could hear a pin drop. Savy turned to us. "Y'all, I want this more than I've ever wanted anything in my life,"

Savy continued. "I'm willing to risk anything, everything . . ."

"It'll be scary," Kimmy warned.

"Yeah," Sandra agreed. "But now we'll be scared together."

It was really happening.

"We need a great name," Savy said eagerly.

"How about the Wild Punch?" Kimmy suggested, punching the air and laughing, "since that's what Brenda was about to throw."

"Or how about the Wild Bunch?" Sandra suggested.

I looked around at those three incredibly cool girls who had stood up for me, and something in my heart felt . . . well, I guess it felt freed. Which I guess is what made me blurt out "How about Wild Hearts?"

They stared at me.

"That's good," Savy said, nodding slowly. "That's really, really good."

"I love it!" Kimmy cried.

"Yeah," Sandra said. "It's sexy and tough."

Kimmy's eyes got huge. "Are we really—"

"We are," Savy confirmed. "We're a band."

"We've got to do originals," I warned. "We don't want to be just some derivative imitation band."

"Well, not all originals," Sandra said. "We have to be commercial to really succeed."

"And we'll play a lot of rock," I insisted.

"And country," Savy said.

"But I hate country!" I protested.

"Oy, McVay," Savy groaned.

"Well, I do!" I insisted.

"You only *think* you hate country," Kimmy corrected me mildly.

"But what about classic rock?" I tried. "You know, Elvis, Jerry Lee Lewis—"

"THAT'S COUNTRY!!" all three girls yelled together.

I shot them a look.

"Country rock, how's that?" Savy the peacemaker asked.

I made a face.

"Hey, girls!" Ms. Jacobi called to us from the stage. "We're all heading over to the opening night party, and your families are out in the hall about ready to leave!"

"Okay, we'll table this conversation until tomorrow after school," Savy said. "It'll be our first band meeting."

"For Wild Hearts!" Kimmy said softly, trying out the name.

Wild Hearts.

I was in a new band.

I hurried out to the hall to find my parents and my sister, eager to tell them the news.

And then I stopped.

And the world fell in on me.

How could I have possibly forgotten?

I was grounded. I had to get a part-time job until I earned at least a thousand dollars. There was no way on this green earth that my parents were going to let me be in a band.

Except they had to. That was all. They just had to.

I took a deep breath and headed for them.

"Jane!"

I turned around. It was Kimmy.

"I just wanted to say ... Well, what you told me back there in the music room. It really helped me," she said softly.

"Yeah?" I asked, really pleased. "Because you found out we're not that different after all, huh?"

"Oh, no, we're totally different," Kimmy assured me. "I would die if people quacked when I walked by and spread rumors about me being fast. I would transfer to a private school in a New York minute!"

"Gee, that option never really entered my mind," I replied wryly.

"I just thought you were so brave to tell me the truth," Kimmy continued earnestly. "And I thought . . . well . . . maybe I could be brave, too."

"You were," I said.

"Yeah," Kimmy agreed, as if she had surprised herself. "I was, wasn't I?"

Savy ran over to us. "Y'all, Ms. Jacobi wants all four of us for a photo. Where's Sandra?"

"Here," Sandra said, coming out of the crowd. "I just told my parents about Wild Hearts, and they want to meet you."

"Wild Hearts," Kimmy said, thrilling at the sound of the name.

"That's us," Savy said.

"Let's not congratulate ourselves until we actually rehearse, okay?" Sandra suggested dryly.

"Hey, band!" Ms. Jacobi called to us, spying the four of us together. "Just stand there a sec and let the photographer get your picture!"

"Mush together, y'all," a short guy with braces told us, aiming his camera in our direction.

Savy, Kimmy, Sandra, and I put our arms around each other and obligingly mushed together.

"This is gonna be a great shot!" he decreed, snapping off a photo. "What should I label it? 'Pit band'?"

"Label it 'The incredibly hot girls in Wild Hearts'!" I cried.

"Right!" Savy agreed. "At our very first photo opportunity. This shot is going to be worth a fortune someday!"

We smiled for the camera, our arms around

each other, and I felt, for the very first time since I'd left New York, that maybe I *did* still have a life. A new life.

I was Jane McVay, drummer for Wild Hearts, and there was nothing that would stop me.

Let 'em quack.

We were going to be an awesome band.

Dear Readers,

To all my longtime friends out there who know me from SUNSET ISLAND, and to all my new friends, I want to welcome you to the wonderful world of WILD HEARTS!

I am so excited about this series, and I hope you will be, too. I'm having a blast writing it. First of all, I've fallen in love with Jane, Kimmy, Savy, and Sandra (I only wish I had been as cool and talented as they are when I was in high school!), and I'm also totally psyched to be writing about Nashville, which is my hometown. Since I've had a chance to actually work with such superstars as Garth Brooks and John Mellencamp, and since I used to be a singer myself, it's a lot of fun for me to be writing about a girls' band, a subject I know lots about. I'm telling you, you will be getting the inside scoop! Forget about MTV!

So, listen, I really want to hear from you guys out there, so that I can make this series what you really want it to be! Write to me at the address below. I promise to read and personally answer every single letter I receive. Hey, I figure if you care enough to write, you deserve a letter back! I will also pick a few letters to publish here in the WILD HEARTS MAIL BOX in the back of all future books—so if you want your letter considered for publication, just say so. If your letter is published, I'll send you a free auto-graphed copy of that book.

I always say I have the greatest fans in the world, because it's true. I've received letters from all over the world, and I know how smart, interesting, funny and deep you guys really are. Thank you so much for believing in me, because you know I believe in you.

And remember, I'll keep writing as long as you keep reading!

WILD HEARTS FOREVER!

Cherie Bennett

Cherie Bennett
c/o Archway Paperbacks
Pocket Books
1230 Avenue of the Americas
New York, NY 10020

All letters printed become property of the publisher.

Get a WILD HEARTS Magnet...*FREE!*

Of course you're wild about Cherie Bennett's hot new series *WILD HEARTS!* Now you can get a *free* WILD HEARTS magnet that will look *great* in your locker by:

- filling in the coupon below,
- clipping the half-a-heart from WILD HEARTS and the half from WILD HEARTS ON FIRE (on sale mid-March, 1994) *and*
- mailing all three to:

> Pocket Books
> Dept. WH, 13th Floor
> 1230 Ave of the Americas
> New York, NY 10020

Name (please print clearly)   Birthdate

Street Address

City   State   Zip